THE ALPHABET ARCHIVES

Printed in the United States of America

Printing, 2019, 2017

ISBN 978-0692902219

Ingram Content Group Inc.
1 Ingram Boulevard, La Vergne, Tennessee 37086
(615) 793-5000
IngramContent.com

Preface

I would like to thank all of my friends and family that have supported me since the first installment. As the story continues, you may wonder what's really behind closed doors. Not everything is what it seems to be in today's world. With various corporations, organizations, and companies in existence, there may be a dark side to them.

In Loving Memory of

Ralph William Giovannone (August 26, 1950 - March 28, 2007)

Alberta "Joann" Heeter (January 15, 1926 - January 19, 2014)

Sharon Sue Giovannone Furbee (September 1, 1951 - May 21, 2014)

Sierra Giovannone-Roberts (October 6, 1990 - June 27, 2014)

Donald Leroy "Gio" Giovannone (February 8, 1943 - November 18, 2014)

Introduction

July 22, 2020

There is a man sprinting down a hallway made of concrete and newly paved cement. The walls and floor were the mixes of beige and yellow. There was bright, white lighting on the ceiling as it lit across the hallway. The man was running from a sign of imminent danger. His body image was a mix between a medium and a large build, but muscular and fit for his weight. He was white in skin color and had black, short hair. He was wearing a black T-shirt with blue denim pants and black tennis shoes. His facial expression was aggressive as his eyes were wide and grinned his teeth. He was sprinting so fast that his footsteps can be heard from a distance away, causing him to breathe heavily.

As the man was running towards a door, two agents in business attire come out from doors in both sides holding black assault rifles. They came from brightly lit rooms, emitting white light. The light from the rooms was bright enough to illuminate the floor. The doors closed as the two agents were standing beside each other. The agents' business attire was in all black except for their dress shirt and wore a black tie. The agents are white in skin color. The man stopped running immediately as the agents pointed both guns at him. He continued to breathe heavily. "Give up now, you're only making it worse on yourself," said one of the agents. He just looked at the agents and was only a few feet away at this point. His breathing became calmer.

The man suddenly began charging at the agents and prepared to fight them. He focused on the agent to his right. The agent was about to ready his weapon, but his reaction time was altered. The man grabbed him and pushed him violently against the wall. He has a hold of his dress shirt as he vigorously pulls the agent close to him. He immediately pushes the agent up against the wall. The man turns the agent towards the way of the door the man was running to. He lets the agent go and forcefully clenches his fists. He begins to punch the agent mercilessly. He punched the agent furiously in the head and chest as the agent grunts from the impacts. The man gives a punishing uppercut to his chin.

The other agent tries to intervene by shooting a few rounds at the man, missing him by mere inches. He didn't lose concentration from the bullets as he continued to attack the agent he targeted. He gave the agent a devastating right hook to his cheekbone, killing him on the spot. The agent turned his body and thudded to the ground. He looked down on the agent, giving an aggressive look by widening his eyes, expressing intense rage and breathing heavily. Blood was around the agent's face with several bruises and lacerations.

The man now turns his attention to the other agent. His menacing look brings terror to the agent's eyes, causing him to shake while aiming at him. The man walks up to him and clenches his fists. He hastily pushes the agent's assault rifle to the agent's side right before he was about to pull the trigger. He began punching the agent in the diaphragm, causing him to drop his weapon. The agent grunts and kneels to the ground. The man swiftly kicks the agent against the wall, causing him to fall and lay in pain on the ground. The agent grunted in agony. The man quickly pulled the agent from the ground and instantly snapped his neck. The agent thudded to the ground, dead on the spot. The man slowed down his heavy breathing, but still tense. He looked at both of the dead agents.

The man started walking towards the door ahead of him. The door was beige and had a small screen by its side. It was a hand scanner. He walked back to the agent he first targeted. He grabbed the agent by the arm and hoisted him over his shoulder. He walked back to the door and placed the agent's hand on the scanner. The screen turned neon green as a line appeared from the top of the screen and slowly worked its way down. The line went back up to the top and disappeared. He took the agent and pushed him backward, thudding to the ground. A holographic numeric screen in neon green light suddenly projected with the layout of a telephone. He quickly tapped four numbers to enter the security code of the door. The holographic screen showed the words, ACCESS GRANTED in green lettering. The screen shrank into oblivion after the hand scanner made a strange electronic noise.

He opened the door and began running into the new room as he was on a suspended metallic platform. The room appeared all metallic as the walls were far apart, making it open in the center. The room was constantly lit up by a fluctuating dim red light accompanied by a loud alarm. The platform was steep as it was only a few feet wide and had guardrails. The guardrails prevent anyone from falling down into the seemingly bottomless black pit below. The platform was about fifty feet long.

After running on the platform, he came to a stop on a

bigger, circular platform, but wasn't metallic. He was looking

at a complex computer module that stretched across the

platform. The set up was bulky as it was thick and comprised

hundreds of buttons each emitting a bright hue of yellow.

Above the module was a huge holographic screen that was

about thirty feet tall and fifty feet wide. The screen had a red

outline and displayed two people, showing their faces. They

were Darrell Friegman and Phoenix Leyton.

Four days later...

July 26, 2020

Darrell and Phoenix are running in the back entrance hallway of the cafeteria of B&N Financing. The walls were made of bricks. They quickly glanced behind them to see the agents with their modified weapons sprinting towards them. "Come on, Phoenix!" Darrell yelled.

Darrell and Phoenix charge at the door and see the clear blue skies outside. They run on the sidewalk beside B&N Financing. The shade covered the sun's rays from where they were running. Phoenix quickly looks behind her to see two agents running towards their way from the opposite side of them. "Follow my lead," said Darrell. The agents fire at them with their modified pistols. They shot a couple armor piercing rounds, coming out with intense velocity. The bullets barely missed as they whistled behind them.

Darrell and Phoenix were running to the edge of the building, feeling the sun's rays hitting their bodies. They both began to breathe heavily and become slightly exhausted. "Don't stop, keep moving!" Darrell said, encouraging Phoenix. After running for about a minute, they stop to catch their breath. They stood by a white rectangular object that contained soil inside it, which was made out of marble and was five feet tall. They got caught off guard as they saw a few supercars and other high-performance vehicles in the distance coming towards their way.

The vehicles were fast approaching. There were five vehicles in all, each with a different color. They were yellow, orange, dark red, black, and light blue all in order. Phoenix locked her sight on the yellow vehicle, a modern Ferrari. Her head followed the direction of the car as it drove towards her.

Phoenix took a glance inside the Ferrari to notice the passenger and realized they were agents. Shocked and surprised, she turned her head, looking at Darrell beside her. Darrell sensed that something was wrong. Phoenix could sense faint footsteps coming from behind. She looked behind her to notice the two agents that almost killed them in the cafeteria. The agents started running from the back entrance of the building. They appeared small as they were far away.

Just as Darrell looked behind, he saw the agents from inside the building running behind the two agents already pursuing them. He quickly looked straight to see the traffic ahead of him, "Come on, let's go, come on!"

As Phoenix and Darrell continue running, the agents fired a couple shots. Just before they ran to the left and disappeared from the agents' sight, a barrage of bullets was fired, missing them both by a couple inches. The bullets pierced several holes on a couple of commuting vehicles, causing panic with the occupants inside them. The bullets just made their way through the vehicles' car doors, but didn't injure the drivers.

Darrell and Phoenix cut to their left to run frantically through the roads. They run under the line of trees from the opposite side of B&N Financing's entrance.

Darrell and Phoenix are now running beside the metallic walls of the parking garages of B&N Financing. "In that garage," Darrell said, pointing out its entrance.

They both arrive at the cylindrical steel bolts of the parking lot of Parking Garage B. They stop running as Darrell marks his attention on the digital numeric touchpad beside the bolts. He feverishly typed his work identification number on the touchpad to enter.

While he was waiting for the steel bolts to open, Darrell looked to notice more high-performance vehicles on the road from the distance. The vehicles are turning towards his point of view on the oncoming side, covering all four lanes. Phoenix looked and also noticed several more high-performance vehicles going the speed limit. As they drove closer, all of the vehicles begin to accelerate towards them almost at the same time. They both panicked, waiting for the steel bolts to move. Darrell gets tense as the vehicles came closer. He looked at the steel bolts and yelled, "Come on, fucking open, damn it!"

"Darrell, look!" Phoenix panicked. Darrell looked behind him. The agents on foot finally caught up to them. "Shit!" he said. The agents stopped running and pointed all of their modified firearms at them. There were shotguns, pistols, assault rifles, and machine guns. Darrell and Phoenix just looked at the agents as they were concealing their weapons.

Suddenly, the steel bolts slowly began moving and disappeared into the wall. Darrell and Phoenix quickly turn themselves around to face the bolts. "Let's go!" Darrell said. All of the agents began firing their weapons as Darrell and Phoenix sprint through the parking lot, barely missing them. The agents cease fire as the vehicles drove in their point of view. Phoenix and Darrell run up the stairs to the walking

area and sprint beside the guardrails, searing with adrenaline

and breathing heavily. There was still that eight-inch tall stripe

on the bottom of the wall. After sprinting for about two

minutes, they turn left and run again.

As Darrell and Phoenix enter the parking garage, they're

surprised by an agent holding a modified pistol. He was tan in

skin color and had a small black microphone attached to his

ear. He has a medium build with a wide head and is bald. The

pistol the agent was holding was different. The pistol has a

silver chrome finish with its barrel opening that's the size of a

nickel. The agent jerked his arms and set them straight, firmly

aiming at them. He slowly walks towards them with a

determined face. The agent stops walking when he's a few

feet away from both of them.

Darrell and Phoenix just look at the agent, not giving the

effort to fight back. Phoenix takes a deep breath and looks

down. She lifts her head back, "We give up." She lifted her

arms up. Darrell was surprised from Phoenix's choice of words, but kept his emotions to himself. "It's the end of the line," the agent said while cocking his gun. Phoenix kept looking at the agent while slowly breathing. Darrell slowly moved his head to look at Phoenix. He turns his head again to look at the agent.

Darrell begins to charge at the agent with brute force. He grabs and pulls him, pinning the agent against the wall. Darrell places his arm on the bottom of his neck. The agent's face increases in aggression as his eyes widen. He kicks Darrell in his knee. He charges a punch at Darrell, but he ducked before the agent could execute it. The agent kneed him in the chin, causing his head to slightly jerk backward and almost kneel to the ground. Darrell quickly got back up and clenched his fists. He punched the agent hard in the diaphragm. The agent made an "Oomph!" as his cheeks puffed out. The agent quickly recovered and readied his fists. He grunted and flew one of his fists at Darrell, but Darrell dodged the attack. He charged and performed a left hook to the agent's face, immediately reacting to the impact. The agent recovered to charge at Darrell. Darrell dodged again. He charged with maximum force, performing a right hook. He punched the agent once more in the diaphragm. The agent bent over, grunting from the pain. Darrell performed a final, but punishing left hook, causing the agent to thud to the ground and drop his gun. He attempted to get up on his feet, but was struggling from his bruises.

The agent saw Phoenix slowly walking up to him as the sun illuminated behind her. She looked down with a mix of anger and rage. She immediately crouches down to grab the agent by his suit jacket. She punches the agent in the face, making the agent yell in agony. Phoenix lets go and perform a swift kick to his chest, throwing him down to the ground. The agent cries out, pleading for mercy. Phoenix looks down at the agent with a disgusted look. Her breathing is slow, but heavy. "You're right," Phoenix said, taking a couple steps towards the agent. "This is the end of the line."

Phoenix slowly crouches down to grab the agent's pistol. She violently grabs a hold of the agent and lifts him up. Phoenix cocks the pistol, "And YOU crossed it!" She jerks the agent forward and applies pressure on his chest with the pistol. She pulls the trigger and fires a deafening round, exiting his stomach. The bullet made a hissing sound when the pistol fired, burning in the gunshot. A thick amount of white smoke came out of the barrel of the gun. The agent started to gag and gurgle from the burn. He started to spit out a small amount of blood and collapsed to the ground, laying on his back. The agent died shortly after. Phoenix looked down at the fallen agent angrily, slowly breathing heavily. She looked at the barrel to notice minuscule amounts of boiling hot water. She aimed the pistol at the ground and cocked the gun. Darrell looked at Phoenix in surprise. He shook his head to switch his focus on the agents from outside of the parking lot, "Come on, Phoenix, we have to go!"

Darrell and Phoenix sprint up to the eighth floor of the parking garage.

He spots the parked maroon BMW. They keep running on the walking area until they go down the small steps in the center. "This way," Darrell said. They run to the far side of the parking floor to approach the vehicle. Darrell presses a silver button with an arrow on his car keys to unlock it.

They open the car doors and climb into the vehicle. Darrell puts the keys in the ignition to start the car. The vehicle's engine roared as the interior lights came on. He sets the vehicle in reverse and faced the exit sign. He set the vehicle into drive and propelled their way towards the exit. "What the hell is going on?" Darrell said as he was entering the seventh floor.

"He was right," Phoenix said. Darrell turned his head to look at Phoenix. "Warren said they were building an army." Darrell faces the windshield, thinking about what's going on outside of the parking lot. "The last time was a warm-up. This is only the beginning."

THE ALPHABET ARCHIVES

Chapter 1: Escalation

July 26, 2020

New York City, New York

Darrell is just driving into the parking garage exit. As he approaches the sunlight, he immediately turned to the right to notice the parking lot mostly full of vehicles. He turned towards the direction of the steel bolts of the parking lot exit. The speed of the BMW was steadily increasing as he was approaching the bolts, slowly opening. Darrell drove through the exit just in time after the bolts disappeared.

Darrell entered the road and floored the throttle. He cut off some commuting vehicles, which caused them to quickly brake and screech their tires. A couple drivers beeped their horns at Darrell as he was passing. He saw the agents on foot and a small fleet of vehicles from a distance. The agents on foot shoot at the BMW, leaving several bullet holes on its side, nearly missing Darrell and Phoenix.

Darrell entered a road with buildings on both sides, temporarily escaping the agents pursuing them. He looked shocked as he widened his eyes. "Shit, that was close!" Darrell said in a panic. He heard shooting from the side of the vehicle. "Phoenix, check the side!" She rolled the window down and peeked her head out. "Oh, shit!" Phoenix yelled.

Phoenix noticed that the agents' vehicles caught up to them. They started firing at the BMW, causing more metal to rip. She quickly slips back in the vehicle. "Darrell, keep driving! Don't stop!" she panicked. "Their bullets cut through the metal of the car!" Darrell switches into fourth gear, gradually increasing in speed. Phoenix had to think of a plan. She looked at Darrell, "Okay, here's the plan, we have to get into an alleyway. But for right now, keep driving, we have to keep as much distance from them as possible."

Darrell quickly switches into fifth gear. The pursuing

vehicles continued firing, quickly filling the BMW's rear

bumper with bullet holes. The bullets left just enough

damage to go through the trunk of the vehicle, puncturing its

material.

Darrell turned his head, spotting possible alleyways he

could turn in. His eyes targeted the last alleyway on the side

of the road. He abruptly pushed the brake, leaving a thick trail

of smoke. He didn't completely stop as he slowed the vehicle

to thirty miles per hour.

Darrell quickly turned to drive towards the alleyway and

goes over a sidewalk, cutting more commuters off. He steadily

increased the speed to forty-five miles per hour, trying to buy

time from the agents pursuing them. He steadily slowed

down, but was still driving quickly. "Hang on," Darrell insisted.

"Darrell, what are you doing?!" Phoenix panicked.

"Just trust me. Force your back on the seat. Brace

yourself! This may hurt a little bit."

Darrell and Phoenix force themselves against the seats. He was approaching fast towards a brick wall with a green dumpster on the side. Darrell sucks his chest in and takes his arms away from the steering wheel, "Chest in and arms out!"

"What?!"

"Do it!" Phoenix followed his commands just before the vehicle came in contact with the brick wall. She extended her arms out against the seat. The front of the vehicle immediately took the impact, causing the airbags to deploy. They both jerk forward from the force of the collision. The front of the vehicle was heavily damaged as the front bumper and the hood molded into an irregular shape while also damaging the mirrors.

The airbags started to deflate. Phoenix was shocked as she slowly turned her head to look at Darrell. "Are you crazy?!" Phoenix yelled at the top of her lungs. Darrell began raising his voice, but didn't yell, "Relax, Phoenix. Don't freak out because they'll be driving by at any moment." She gave him a disgusted look.

Darrell just looked at Phoenix, not giving in to her expression. "Alright, here's the plan," he said. Phoenix still kept her expression. "They're going to think we're dead when they pass by." He was improvising as he was looking at the steering wheel and the window beside Phoenix, "We're going to play dead. I need you to watch and look for the vehicles. Watch the side mirror and pretend you're dead." Phoenix took her head and leaned against the window and kept her eyes on the side mirror. Darrell simply placed his head on the steering wheel, facing the airbag. Phoenix saw the vehicles slowly driving past the alleyway. The vehicles were far enough to not notice her movement. Phoenix saw nothing but vehicles in the side mirror for ten seconds. "They passed, they're going to turn and drive past us again," Darrell said.

"Close your eyes," Darrell whispered. Phoenix closed her eyes and tried her best not to move a muscle. The vehicles were now closer to them as they were passing by. They were

going slower than when they were further away from them to

take precaution. Right before the vehicles passed, Phoenix

was slowly breathing and moved her eyes under her eyelids,

but was barely noticeable. The agents looked at them,

convincing themselves that they are dead.

After about twenty seconds, Phoenix opens her eyes

cautiously. There were no more vehicles in sight. "We're

clear," Phoenix said. They climbed out of the vehicle with

Phoenix still holding her pistol. "What do we do now?" Darrell

said.

"We have to find a new vehicle." They looked at the

vehicle's car doors to see the damage. Several dents were

scattered all around the doors. They began running towards

the short path of the alleyway from where the agents were

previously driving.

As they were towards the edge, Phoenix stopped running

and let her arm out to stop Darrell. She firmly looked at him and whispered, "Shh, be quiet. There may be someone out there still." Phoenix leaned up against the brick wall. She quickly waved her hand towards herself, "Darrell, up against the wall." He quietly walked up to the wall and placed his back against it. Phoenix aimed the pistol down to the ground with both hands. "You wanted me to be the watchdog," she said.

Phoenix slowly walked sideways against the wall. She got on the edge and peeked her head out to see what's out there. No agents were present, but she noticed an unsupervised vehicle from a distance. It was a motorcycle. She kept her head out for a few seconds to take precaution. She looked at Darrell, "I'm going to go out. Stay here. Try not to make a sound." Phoenix took the pistol and placed it in her pocket.

"What's going on?" Darrell asked. Phoenix went out before she could answer his question. She quickly lifted her shirt up and covered the pistol to conceal it. As she moved from the alleyway, she began jogging on the sidewalk. She was taking precaution while jogging towards the motorcycle. She saw that the roads aren't as congested as there were a couple commuting vehicles coming towards her way at a time.

After jogging for a couple minutes, Phoenix was close enough to the motorcycle. She slowed down, then stopped and leaned up against a window of a small department store. In front of the window was a couple white mannequins wearing women's clothing, which included short sleeve shirts and navy blue denim jeans. She peeked her head towards the silver metallic edge of the department store.

As Phoenix brings her head out more, she noticed a white skin colored agent standing beside the motorcycle, but didn't notice her. The agent had short, black hair and was holding a black assault rifle. She became tense and leaned back against the window. She started to get frustrated and breathed heavily. She calmed herself down by slowing her breathing.

Phoenix took the pistol out of her pocket and slowly began walking towards the agent. The agent looked at Phoenix and became alert by lifting his firearm. She fired a round at the agent's stomach, causing him to drop his weapon. The bullet burned through as there was a small amount of smoke coming out of his back. The barrel emitted a thick trail of white smoke with a couple drops of boiling water. The agent thudded to the ground, motionless.

She put the pistol back in her pocket and walked to the agent's dead body. She crouched down to grab his assault rifle. She noticed a black sling on the assault rifle extending to the rear of the gun. After she took the weapon, she stood up and hoisted it on her back with the sling over her shoulder.

Phoenix looked to see the motorcycle. It was rather sleek in appearance. The paint was silver as its finish was in chrome except for the tires. She realized that the motorcycle's manufacturer was from the Austrian company, KTM. The manufacturer's name was on its skirts on both sides, which the name was in black. The motorcycle was covered with metal plates that matched the shapes of its body frame. The small plates were held together by several nuts and bolts. Above the motorcycle's speedometer was a portable, silver machine gun mounted onto the center of it. Both of the vehicle's handlebars extended to about eight inches.

Phoenix runs to the motorcycle to check for the keys, but the keys were not in the ignition. She runs back to the dead agent and crouches down to his side. She scrambles as she searches the agent's pocket for the keys, but nothing was found. She stood up and leaped her leg over the opposite side and crouched down again. She searched the agent's other pocket to feel something that's made of metal. Phoenix pulled out the contents to reveal a set of keys. She looked down at the agent in frustration, "Smart bastard."

Phoenix stood up and ran back to the motorcycle with the keys and pistol in hand. She quickly hopped on only to notice an orange supercar in the distance. She immediately starts the motorcycle as its modified engine made a loud scream.

Phoenix set the motorcycle into first gear by pressing a padlock button on the right handle. She noticed that the supercar was quickly accelerating away from her. She immediately floors it, forcing her to press her legs in between the vehicle. The quick acceleration caused the motorcycle to perform a small wheelie. The motorcycle's engine grew louder while being accompanied by a whistling sound from its performance enhancements. She quickly shifts to second gear, accelerating to sixty miles per hour in just under three seconds. Phoenix's vision started to get blurry as she saw the buildings on both sides. The supercar was accelerating at the same rate as Phoenix. The blistering acceleration forced her to lean towards the front of the bike. Commuting vehicles were quickly coming towards her way, so she overtakes the vehicles without leaning too far on either side.

Phoenix was catching up to the supercar as she shifts to

third gear, climbing up to a hundred miles per hour. She maintains her balance as she runs through a red light, cutting off multiple drivers. After she exited a four-way intersection, she entered into another road with buildings on both sides with varying heights.

Phoenix quickly turned to the right, narrowly missing a commuting driver ahead of her. She turned onto the last lane of the road, which was the same lane that the supercar is on. She could hear the supercar's loud V12 engine whistling across the road. Phoenix pressed on with full throttle in an attempt to tailgate the supercar. She shifted into fourth gear, skyrocketing to a hundred and forty miles per hour.

Phoenix is getting closer to the supercar as she is about fifty feet away. She continued to press on as she was halfway through the fourth gear. She's nearly ten feet away from it now. She was able to catch a glimpse of the vehicle's manufacturer on the rear bumper. It was under the Italian company, Lamborghini.

Phoenix just passed the rear taillights of the

Lamborghini. She reduced pressure on the throttle as she is

now facing right beside the supercar. The agent driving the

supercar turns his head to Phoenix. She notices two smooth

metallic adjusters with one on each handlebar of the

motorcycle. The adjusters are connected to a gun. She takes

the adjuster on the left handlebar and applies pressure to it.

Phoenix moves the adjuster to the far end of the handlebar.

This made the gun move to the right, aiming at the supercar's

side mirror.

Phoenix looked to face the driver, giving an infuriated

look. She presses a silver rectangular button on the left

handlebar of the motorcycle. It triggered the gun to fire at an

alarming rate. The window of the supercar was taking

minimal damage due to its strong resistance. The bulletproof

glass was strong enough to resist up to a .30 caliber cartridge.

The window starts to take on more damage as its texture

changed to the color of snow, forming several tiny cracks.

Phoenix continued to fire as the bullets slowly pierced through the glass. The glass was growing weaker as the bullets continued to penetrate. The glass began to reveal two agents as it collapsed from the passenger side.

Phoenix ceased fire for only a short moment. While she hesitated, the driver pulled out the same kind of pistol she used earlier. Before the agent could pull the trigger, she started firing the weapon again. The bullets went right through the agents' heads, causing blood to splatter on the other window and on the seats. The passenger leaned his motionless body towards the broken glass on his side. The driver leaned forward, almost touching the steering wheel. The Lamborghini began to slow down drastically, causing the tires to screech loudly and leave a thick trail of smoke. Phoenix quickly decelerates beside the vehicle as she was braking hard, causing the tires to leave a trail of black tar on the asphalt.

The Lamborghini came to a complete stop. Phoenix was

about ten feet away from the vehicle by the time she stopped. She got off and ran towards the supercar. Commuting vehicles were coming towards her way, but were from a far distance.

Phoenix opened the car door as it extended upward like a gullwing. She noticed that the driver had his foot on the brake. She unbuckled the seat belt of the dead driver and forcefully dragged him out. She let go as he thudded to the ground. She noticed the car was still in drive. She quickly pushed on the brake to set it in park. Phoenix ran to the other side of the vehicle and pulled the passenger out. The passenger thudded to the ground. She closed the passenger door and ran back to the driver's side. There were small blood stains on top of the black seats.

Phoenix climbed into the vehicle and closed the door. She noticed several differences on the dashboard and interior. This wasn't an average Lamborghini that's found in the automotive market. There were buttons that scattered around the dashboard, but Phoenix couldn't tell what the buttons were for. She noticed paddle shifters with one on each side behind the steering wheel. The buttons were black as there were alternating colors of neon glow in the center of them. "Hope Darrell likes this one," Phoenix said to herself.

Phoenix shifted the Lamborghini down four times until it was in first gear. She slowly let her foot on the throttle and quickly turned. Phoenix went over a divider while crossing over, causing the vehicle to shake for a brief moment. She turned left to straighten the vehicle on the other side of the road. Phoenix's body started to feel lighter as she began to accelerate. She shifts to second gear as she was overtaking someone ahead of her.

Phoenix drives through the four-way intersection while running a red light. She continued accelerating until she was going about a hundred miles per hour. She abruptly stopped the vehicle and turned to drive on the road of the department store.

Darrell was still beside the battered BMW as he was waiting for Phoenix. He took a big sigh in frustration and raised his voice, "What the hell are you doing, Phoenix?!"

Darrell heard an engine of a vehicle. As the sound grew louder, he saw an orange sharp-looking supercar with broken glass. He saw Phoenix inside as she was stopping at the alleyway. He was shocked from the damage of the windows. Phoenix makes a loud whistle and yells, "What do you think?" Darrell raises his eyebrows in surprise and question as his mouth drops. Phoenix said while moving her arm towards her and smiles, "Well, come on, what are you waiting for?"

Darrell starts walking to the Lamborghini. Phoenix opens the gullwing door and walks to the passenger door. "And you're taking the wheel," Phoenix insisted. Darrell looked at Phoenix in confusion. "Just get in the car, I'll explain later," she said quickly and firmly. Darrell wanted to question her, but couldn't argue and said, "Okay." He ran around the front bumper and faced the driver's side. He opened the driver's door and climbed into the vehicle as Phoenix followed.

As Darrell and Phoenix closed their doors, he noticed the several buttons scattered around the dashboard and interior. Each button had a different purpose. He was amazed by the interior as he noticed the instrument cluster. The cluster was all digital as the center console included a small touchscreen on the top of it. The console was also accompanied by a series of buttons that are connected to the touchscreen and the vehicle overall. Above the touchscreen was another screen that projected what's behind the vehicle. Darrell looked at Phoenix in disbelief, "How the hell did you get a hold of this?"

"It wasn't easy. I worked my ass off just to get this damn thing. That's why there are a couple blood stains on the seats."

"What's with all of these buttons? What do you think the organization's planning?"

"Look around it, Darrell. This isn't your average car." He

looked at the buttons around the interior once more, but more closely. The words on most of the buttons represented several strategical and tactical functions that could be used for emergency operations. "It's also a weapon."

Chapter 2: The Weapon's Edge

Darrell immediately started driving on the road. He drives in a straight line and the vehicle accelerated quickly. The vehicle steadily increased to sixty miles per hour, fifteen miles over the speed limit. Darrell turned and drove in between buildings on both sides. "So, what's going on? How are we on the run again?" Darrell questioned. Phoenix took out her modified pistol while looking down at the seat, "Like I said, Darrell. Last year was just a warm-up. They're building an army. I was afraid this day would come."

"What are you trying to say, Phoenix? Could this be the

start of a war?"

"Maybe, but I can't really say that for sure."

"Then, why are they waiting?"

"Like you said, they could be planning something."

Darrell and Phoenix take a glimpse to see what's behind them. He notices several vehicles slowly turning from his perspective in the rear-view mirror from a distance. Phoenix rolls the damaged window down and peers her head out, looking in the side mirror. More vehicles keep turning as it becomes a fleet. The vehicles covered most of the lanes.

Phoenix was getting tense. She put her head back in the vehicle and crouched in the seat to take cover. She looks at Darrell seriously and firmly says slowly, "Whatever you do, do not accelerate." Darrell takes a couple deep breaths and glances in the rear-view mirror, "Look at all of those vehicles."

"Well, we both know that they want us dead. With that many vehicles involved, they could strike at any moment." Phoenix firmly tells Darrell, "Here's what we're going to do.

When they go full throttle, accelerate. Hard." The vehicles are still keeping their pace with Darrell and Phoenix. "They probably think we're one of them."

Phoenix looked in the side mirror. She noticed that the vehicles began to accelerate. She slipped her head back in the vehicle and panicked, "Shit, they saw us!" Phoenix readied at her pistol, "Accelerate now!"

Darrell looked in the rear-view mirror. He notices that the vehicles were approaching fast. He floors the throttle and shifts to second gear. The vehicle accelerated to a hundred miles per hour in about two seconds. Darrell and Phoenix's bodies felt lighter as the world suddenly blurred around them. "Good choice, Phoenix," Darrell said, complimenting the vehicle.

"Getting this vehicle was the least of my worries." Phoenix cocks the pistol and looks in the side mirror, "Because if it's a war they want, it's a war they'll get." The vehicles draw in closer as they are about a hundred feet away.

Darrell drifted as he and Phoenix felt its impressively responsive handling. Six of the eight pursuing vehicles in the first row began shooting rapid-fire weapons. A couple bullets hit the Lamborghini, but reflected them, creating only small dents. Darrell straightened the vehicle and immediately accelerates. "I didn't even feel the bullets," Darrell said, surprised.

The pursuing vehicles quickly drifted as they both saw the number of vehicles growing. They estimated at least thirty vehicles. Darrell looked at the vehicles in his rear view mirror, angry and frustrated. Phoenix looked in the side mirror. Something snapped in her head, "The buttons!" She slipped her head back in and looked at all of the buttons surrounding the dashboard. "Darrell, use the buttons!" Most of the buttons had a different weapon assigned to each of them.

Darrell pressed a button on the left side just above of the center console that said MACHINE GUNS. He then pressed a button that said REAR on the air vents above the center

console. They looked at the rear-view camera screen above

the center console. Phoenix pointed her finger at the two

vehicles in the center of the lanes. On the screen, it showed

two vehicles, which were yellow and orange. "Focus on those

two vehicles. I'm going to try to take on the red car by the

side mirror," Phoenix said.

Darrell taps the yellow supercar on the screen. The

screen presented a red, circular reticle covering around the

vehicle and showed the words, LOCK ON. As Darrell tapped the

car on the screen again, four lines went into the center of the

reticle in cardinal directions.

Two small flaps of the rear bumper opened upward as

four machine guns came out of the Lamborghini. There were

two guns on each side. The guns quickly turned to the yellow

supercar to lock on to it. The vehicle was a Ferrari.

Darrell noticed two black buttons on the steering wheel

with one on each side. The screen above the center console

displayed the words, WEAPONS READY, catching his attention. He looked at the buttons again and hesitated for a brief moment. He quickly regained his focus as he pressed the black buttons.

The machine guns fired with intense velocity at the Ferrari. The Lamborghini's machine guns are creating damage, but it's not substantial. They only made small dents on the Ferrari's front bumper and hood. The damage didn't affect its performance. Phoenix fires one round at the red supercar, but there was no significant damage. The pursuing vehicles continue to accelerate as they approach Darrell and Phoenix. "Darrell, step on it, they're drawing in!" Phoenix yelled.

"Damn it, why aren't they budging?!" Darrell yelled, frustrated. The yellow and orange vehicles opened small flaps on the front bumper of their vehicles. Two machine guns come out of the openings in each of the vehicles. They fire at the Lamborghini. Just like the yellow supercar, no significant damage, just dents.

Darrell looked at the buttons again above the center console. By MACHINE GUNS, there was a button with a picture of a shield with a zigzag line going down its center. He pressed it as it emitted a blue light. He took a deep breath and focused on the steering wheel. He quickly pressed the buttons and continued firing the machine guns.

The rounds came out rapidly as they were in a different shape. They each had a sharp tip as they did more damage than the regular rounds. The rounds enlarged the dents of the Ferrari, creating small holes on its front bumper and hood. The Ferrari was still going strong. The vehicle's engine is located in its rear. The Ferrari and the orange muscle car, a Dodge, fire their weapons at the Lamborghini. The Lamborghini began to form more dents, but no significant damage.

Darrell noticed a button resembling a horseshoe magnet beside the broken shield button. He pressed it as it emitted a red light and heard clanging in the back. Two of the machine guns moved closer to each other. The other two machine guns moved outward from the vehicle's edge as the other moved inward. All of the guns were still locked on the yellow supercar.

Darrell continues firing at the Ferrari as the bullets intersect. The bullets start attaching to each other, forming a sharper and larger projectile that doubles in size. The Ferrari took excessive damage as the bullets pierce through the front bumper, like burning a hole through fabric. The bullets just barely ripped through the interior of the Ferrari.

Darrell locked on to the driver and passenger of the Ferrari by tapping their bodies on the target screen. The machine guns made clanging noises as they moved upward to target the windshield. The bullets created large holes, quickly traveling through the agent's bodies. Their bodies jumped around in their seats as the bullets pierced through them.

The Ferrari began to slow down as the vehicle behind it gained speed. Darrell shot at both of the Ferrari's front tires, causing it to fly in the air and perform a series of barrel rolls.

The vehicle flew over the fleet as it hit the ground with brute

force, totaling the vehicle. Behind the Ferrari was a navy blue

sports car, which was from the German manufacturer,

Gumpert. The Gumpert accelerates as it takes the place of

the Ferrari.

The Dodge and the Gumpert accelerate to Darrell and

Phoenix. The vehicles shoot their machine guns at the

Lamborghini. Phoenix looked back to see the two vehicles.

She looked tense as she turned back around to face the

windshield, "We need to find some place to cool down."

Darrell continues accelerating as he shifts into fourth

gear, reaching a hundred and eighty miles per hour. He pulls

out the emergency brake and drifts into another road. The

two vehicles kept firing as Darrell was drifting.

The navy blue and orange vehicles were just drifting into

Darrell's direction as they were about fifty feet away. The rest

of the fleet was also turning as they are farther from the

other two pursuing vehicles. They continued firing at the Lamborghini. Darrell quickly turned into another road, which was lined with trees and bushes on the side. Darrell and Phoenix were also driving past a lake. He lowered the vehicle into third gear to increase acceleration efficiency. He floored it as he was overtaking the commuting vehicles ahead of him. He was driving on slight curves on the road from both directions.

Darrell and Phoenix head into another part of town, forming shade underneath the vehicle. They realized they are around the ground of Riverside Park. He decelerated, breathing heavily and taking caution. As he was approaching another road, the fleet showed up in the rear-view mirror, but appeared small. Phoenix looked in the side mirror to see the fleet fast approaching. "Take the right!" she yelled.

Darrell entered another road as the bullets whistled past the vehicle. The road he was on had vehicles parked on both sides. He accelerated on a slightly hilly road. "Take the next right, that might buy us time," Phoenix said. He turned as he steadily accelerated. "Keep your speed down, they might know where we are." While Darrell drives through a four-way intersection, he notices the fleet driving on a different city block, but the fleet didn't see him.

After about a half of a mile of driving, Darrell hung a left into another four-way intersection. They were heading towards a metro station away from the roads. "We'll take that metro station," Darrell said.

Darrell and Phoenix notice a dark tunnel containing train tracks with graffiti on the top. There was fencing by the left side of the tunnel. He turns the headlights on as he enters the tunnel. The interior immediately lights up as all of the buttons and interfaces illuminate. "Let's try to find a resting spot. We need to think of a plan," Darrell insisted.

The Lamborghini's tires were the mix of performance and all-terrain tires. Darrell was driving on the train tracks, making the vehicle rumble. He yawed to the left to enter the smooth part of the tracks to reduce noise. He noticed a source of light from the ceiling after every hundred feet of driving.

Darrell slowed down until he came to a complete stop. He set the vehicle into park. Him and Phoenix opened the gullwing doors and climbed out of the vehicle. They walked up to the front of the vehicle and stood face to face. Phoenix still had the pistol in her hand. She looked at Darrell firmly. "We can't hold them off by ourselves," Darrell said.

"We already took down a vehicle. What makes you say that?"

"Everything has a limit, Phoenix. The vehicle's weapons may be limited."

"Then we need to conserve our ammo. We can rest here and wait out at night. We'll have to get more ammo if needed."

Darrell was getting frustrated, "Phoenix, how the hell are we supposed to fend off these men in black with regular ammo?! We both know that regular ammo is pretty much rendered useless against these crazy bastards!"

"What about before? The car we took down earlier!"

"It doesn't matter, we need to take precaution. We can't just waste our ammo!"

Phoenix was starting to get angry and yelled, "Oh, okay, you think you suddenly know it all, huh? Apparently, you don't remember that I saved your ass from getting killed by that psycho about a year ago!"

"We're both in this mess, Phoenix! They're after both of us now! We can't sit around for too long like fucking tunnel rats! They'll find us eventually!"

Phoenix was infuriated with Darrell and says quietly, "Do you know how much I saved your life, Darrell? I know more than you do when it comes to me and this fucking organization! I knew about it since the day my damn husband was involved." She was starting to increase tension. "You think you know? Think again." The emotional pain was seeping back into Phoenix. "Ever since Warren disappeared, I couldn't stand looking at myself. I would look in the mirror, disgusted and violated."

Darrell looked at Phoenix as he was disgusted from her yelling at him. She took a deep breath and looked down at the ground in guilt. She started calming down. "Darrell?" Phoenix said, lifting her head up. Darrell didn't respond. "Whatever happened, happened. I'm just mad at myself for not saving Warren and I regret it." Darrell lifted his disgusted look off of his face. "And I'm sorry that I took it out on you. You didn't kill him."

Darrell started to show his softer side, "Phoenix, listen to me. It's not your fault, but it happened. You and I got in this mess together. Nothing will bring him back no matter how many agents we kill." Phoenix was feeling calmer as she listened to Darrell. "You can't let your guard down now. They're after us again, and we have to fight. Think about how Warren has impacted your life in good terms. That's what matters, Phoenix."

"I promised him that I'll find a way to bring an end to this."

"Then, what are we waiting for?" Let's go and take these guys down!"

Darrell heard a loud engine sound coming from the beginning of the tunnel. He looked at the tunnel's entrance to locate the sound. "What?" Phoenix questioned. Darrell put his finger to his lips and whispered, "Shh, listen." She looked towards where Darrell was looking. "They might have found us," he assumed.

An indigo-colored vehicle was driving straight and was coming in close to them as it was accelerating. Darrell panicked and said, "Oh, shit." The vehicle was getting closer as the engine grew louder. He caught a small glimpse of the vehicle as it flew past them. He noticed it was a supercar from Nissan. "They didn't stop," Darrell was surprised. The vehicle was driving away from them as it was turning left, disappearing in the distance. Darrell panicked, "We have to follow that vehicle! Come on!"

Darrell and Phoenix quickly get into the Lamborghini as he starts the vehicle, revving its loud, V12 engine. The tires screeched after he sets it in drive. The vehicle quickly accelerates as they follow the Nissan's path, stepping back in the pursuit.

Chapter 3: Meet and Greet

Darrell shifts into second gear as the tunnel blurred around him. He turned left to see a small light emitting from a distance, indicating the end of the tunnel. He notices the indigo Nissan, but continues to drive on.

As Darrell was driving closer, the sunlight was still present as the skies were clear. The tracks were about fifty feet from the ground. He noticed the Nissan turning right to drive off of the tracks, entering ground level. Darrell and Phoenix were surprised. "That person must be up to something," Phoenix said.

After the Nissan drove off, Darrell and Phoenix saw a white train speeding past them. After the train passed, Phoenix heard another train, but it was coming from behind. Darrell looked down to see the navy blue and orange vehicles scouting on a straight road. She looked in her side mirror to see the train getting closer behind them. "Darrell, get off the tracks!" she yelled. He looked in his side mirror and panicked. He immediately drove off the tracks as the Lamborghini high-revved to ground level.

As the vehicle touched ground level, Phoenix looked in her side mirror to see the Nissan make a one hundred and eighty degree turn to face the direction Darrell is driving. Darrell kept his focus on the navy blue and orange vehicles. Phoenix looked back to face the windshield, "Get those two, first. The Nissan's after us now."

Darrell pressed the button that read FRONT, next to REAR, and activated the same weapons he used on the Ferrari. He locked his targets on both vehicles on the target screen after the flaps opened and revealed the machine guns. After the screen projected the words, TARGETS LOCKED, the machine guns separated and reconnected to form an intersection. He could hear the weapons whistle as they move, also following the targets.

Darrell fired at the vehicles as they immediately reacted to the damage. The magnetism of the thick armor-piercing bullets provided increased velocity, making large holes into the targets' rear bumpers. The vehicles eventually gave way to the bullets, popping their tires, and leaving trails of smoke. He continued firing as the vehicles begin to spin out of control. They spun in opposite directions as they impacted the walls of the buildings on both sides, rendering them useless.

Phoenix noticed that the Nissan quickly turned to the left, disappearing, "Shit!"

"What?" Darrell said.

"The Nissan's gone!" Phoenix looked in the rear-view

mirror to see the fleet of vehicles from a far distance. "Better get a move on, we're going to have to use a different strategy against them!" she said.

Darrell looked at the buttons above the center console to notice different choices of weapons. He paid attention to the button that said SNIPER RIFLE. He pressed the button along with another that has a picture of a flame, emitting a red light, and a button that said, SEMI-AUTO. A large flap opened in the center of the rear bumper with a large firearm extending out of the vehicle. There were eight vehicles aligned in a row as they were accelerating towards his way. He locked his aim on one vehicle at a time.

As Darrell prepared to fire, the bullets from the sniper rifle came out with intense velocity, breaking the sound barrier. The bullets were traveling through the air as it followed one of the targets, which was a dark green vehicle. The bullet put a hole through the pursuer's front bumper. He fired at the vehicle's front tires, causing it to lose control and fly up in the air. Darrell locked onto another target, which was a blue vehicle. He fired at it, sharing the same fate as the other one.

As the fleet was drawing towards Darrell, he notices a couple more buttons below the weapons beside the center console. He pressed the button, ARMOR LEVEL 1 while the fleet was shooting at them. Darrell activated the mild armory system. He heard grinding and the clanking of metal as the Lamborghini's exterior was slowly being covered with small padded, orange armor. The vehicle appeared like new, but reinforced. He switched back to MACHINE GUNS along with his preferred settings and fired at the fleet. "This should hold us off for a while," Darrell said.

While being pursued, they notice the Nissan from earlier drifting beside them. They notice a man with short, black hair behind the wheel. "Who is this asshole?" Phoenix said. The Nissan didn't display even a minimal amount of danger.

"I don't know, Phoenix, but he's not indicating a threat.

Maybe he's being hunted, too." The Nissan and Lamborghini travel at matching speeds as if they are in a street race. The fleet was slowly chipping away small fragments of the armor plating of the Lamborghini as two vehicles keep their fire. Darrell tensed up and fired at the two vehicles, green and yellow, locking on both of them, shaking them out of the fleet. He shifts into fifth gear, climbing up to almost two hundred miles per hour, but the fleet was still maintaining distance. "Darrell, drive faster, they're too close!" Phoenix panicked.

"The acceleration's slowing. I can't get it to go any faster." Like the Lamborghini, the Nissan takes down two vehicles with machine guns. Darrell pressed ARMOR LEVEL 2 under ARMOR LEVEL 1 to activate a modified set of armor similar to the vehicle's applied set. He could hear the metal of the vehicle screeching as it is connecting together. Small black plates of metal slowly covered the entire vehicle. Darrell and Phoenix were startled as the metal grew louder. "What the hell is going on?" Darrell said.

Phoenix was shocked as she noticed the Nissan going through the same process. Darrell noticed a button on the bottom of the center console with a black flap covering it. He opened the flap to reveal a red button with a picture of a nitrous bottle. They looked down at the button. "Hang on," Darrell said, holding his breath.

As he activated the nitrous, the vehicle suddenly went into an instant burst of acceleration. This caused them to lean their bodies back against the vehicle from the shift of gravitational force. They were grunting as their bodies felt lighter. The world blurred around them as the vehicle's interior and the target screen were the only objects in focus. Darrell was driving at rapid speeds as he was going neck and neck with the Nissan. He shifted into sixth gear, climbing up to over two hundred and forty miles per hour. He quickly locked on the vehicles behind him and resumed firing the machine guns. He was able to take down three vehicles on the target screen as the Nissan also took down the same amount. The pursuing vehicles flew in the air by reacting to the impact. Darrell deactivated the vehicle's nitrous system by pressing the button to conserve its reserves.

As Darrell and the Nissan were gaining distance from the fleet, he pressed SNIPER RIFLE along with a button showing six circles beside the flame button and SEMI-AUTO. The sniper rifle came out of the Lamborghini as Darrell pressed the black buttons on the steering wheel. The fleet fired at the Nissan and the Lamborghini, but barely made a dent on the armor.

Darrell locked on the two of the remaining row of vehicles and began firing. The bullet dispersed into six small fragments as it traveled with extreme velocity from the heat seeker effect. The two vehicles immediately felt the impact after the fragments ate through their front wheelbase. They flew in the air and fell to the ground, totaling the vehicles.

Darrell switches back to the machine guns with his preferred settings and locked on the next row of vehicles. Darrell and the Nissan fire as they steadily pick off the fleet one by one with armor-piercing bullets. During the ordeal, a couple of the pursuing vehicles spun out of control and impact the buildings' walls between them, damaging the vehicles beyond repair.

Phoenix notices the Nissan changing weapons as she sees the center of its rear bumper switching them. The weapon appeared to be a large silver shotgun. She is shaking from the pull of the Lamborghini's intense feat of speed and says, "He has a shotgun, you better be ready for this, Darrell!" He is still tense while controlling the vehicle.

The Nissan fired one round with a fast rate at the fleet in mid-range. The bullet was rather large as it was appeared to be the size of a .40 caliber. The bullet created a small explosion as it impacted one of the vehicles. The explosion caused excessive damage and a chain reaction, causing a couple other vehicles to react from the blast. Phoenix was shocked by the devastation, "Darrell, step on it!"

"I'm working on it!" They heard another explosion as it destroys a few other vehicles, causing a chain reaction of vehicles spinning out of control and several wall impacts, totaling them. The Nissan shot another round at the three remaining vehicles. The middle vehicle immediately went up in flames as the vehicles between it reacted to the impact, spinning out of control. Phoenix was amazed as she watched the Nissan released pillage on the fleet, "Holy shit!" There were no more vehicles pursuing them.

The Nissan begins to decelerate. "Stop the vehicle!" Phoenix yelled. Darrell slams on the brake as the vehicle begins to decelerate. The sudden amount of deceleration causes their bodies to lean forward as they try to keep themselves in the seats. The tar from the Lamborghini's tires formed skid marks while leaving a thick trail of smoke.

Darrell brought the vehicle to a complete stop. Him and Phoenix were breathing heavily from the sudden chain of events. They looked at each other in awe. He deactivated the armor system as the armor plating slipped back into the vehicle as the Nissan did the same. They quickly unbuckled their seat belts and got out.

Darrell and Phoenix walked towards the rear bumper of their vehicle and towards the Nissan. They notice a man coming out and closes the door. The man looked at both of them with his arms crossed. He had a large, muscular build while wearing a black T-shirt, blue denim jeans, and black tennis shoes.

Phoenix walked in a fast pace towards the man as Darrell was right behind her. They are now standing face to face with the man. "Looks like you guys need some help," the man paused. "And some answers."

"Who the hell are you?" Phoenix questioned.

"I ain't the only one that's being hunted."

"I can see that, but that doesn't fully explain who you are!" Phoenix points the pistol at the man, growing impatient. The man didn't flinch, "Before you pull that trigger, I suggest you calm down before you make things worse for yourself, miss." Phoenix was disgusted as she applied pressure to the pistol.

She noticed a black and silver wristband on the man's arm, easily catching its metallic texture. The man taps the small screen on the wristband. The screen projected a holograph that showed another man's face that was medium in size and was white in skin color. Darrell and Phoenix assumed the man on the holographic screen was a mechanic. The mechanic was wearing a bright orange baseball cap with a couple smears of grease on his cheeks. The screen was glowing against the man's face. The mechanic said in a mellow, yet firm voice, "What's going on?"

"I was chased again, found two. They don't seem to be a threat," the man said.

"Then, why is the woman holding a gun at you?"

"Don't worry about it. They just want answers."

"Alright, I need you to head back over here before they find you again."

"Alright, but give me a minute. I need to talk to these

guys."

"Make it quick, there's no time to sit around."

"Alright, Russell out." The holographic screen disappears back into the wristband.

The man firmly looks at Darrell and Phoenix, "There's no time to negotiate right now, but I'll tell you where we can meet up."

"Him and I need to know. We're the next targets against these damn people," Phoenix said, referring to Darrell after she lowered her weapon.

"I'll give you the coordinates so you can find me." The man taps on the wristband again and taps on the holographic screen to display a three- dimensional map of a city that's far from New York City. "I'm going to be driving down to Los Angeles. There's going to be a warehouse where I'll discuss more details."

"How are we going to keep in contact with you?" said Darrell. Phoenix quickly looks at Darrell with a firm expression and then back to the man.

"In that vehicle of yours, you have to press a button to activate the universal electronic communications. You have to type the person's name in order to communicate. The organization's stepping up their game as their technology advances." Darrell was confused, "Wait, how would you know about the organization?" Phoenix looked at the man with frustration, but the man didn't react to her expression. "Sir, you'll find out soon enough. Like I said, there's no time to explain right now."

"You better explain by the time we get there." Phoenix pauses as her expression changes to anger, "And you better not be hiding something."

"And my name's Russell. Russell Arkwright," the man said, lifting his arm out for a hand shake.

"I'm Phoenix, but I'm not in the mood to shake hands," she refused.

"Actually, I'm not the kind of person that does the meet

and greet anyway." Russell walks back to his car and climbs

into his vehicle. He slowly drives off and takes a left in the

distance.

Darrell and Phoenix walk back to their vehicle and get in.

"So, I guess we have our leads," he said as they were buckling

their seat belts. He starts the vehicle and takes off.

"But why would he want us to meet him in Los Angeles?"

Phoenix questioned while Darrell was accelerating to the

speed limit, which was fifty-five miles per hour.

"Don't know, maybe L.A. could be where they're hiding

out at." Phoenix looked down at her pistol and said, "We have

to be careful with what we're going up against. We just met

the guy, Darrell."

"But maybe he could help us, maybe he understands

what's going on." Darrell took the same left Russell made.

"Maybe, but I don't think I'll be putting all of my eggs in

one basket. We're back in the fight and we have to watch out

for each other."

"And we're going to need to keep in touch as much as possible. I'm going to need your cell phone number."

"We'll deal with that later, focus on the road."

"Even though we killed several people and may get charged with several counts of-"

"Just drive before I get pissed off."

Darrell taps the screen at the top of the center console to turn it on. On the left side in the middle of the center console, he presses a button with a satellite tower emitting transmission waves as it flashes green afterward. The screen shows a layout of a digital yellow QWERTY keyboard. He was surprised by what the screen projected. "This is new," he said to himself. He began typing Russell's first and last name on the screen, with the keys inverting their colors. After Darrell typed Russell's name, him and Phoenix sit back and relax while preparing to travel to the city of Los Angeles.

Chapter 4: The Meetup

July 28, 2020

Downtown Los Angeles, California

Darrell and Phoenix are traveling on a straight road at midnight. They were almost out of gas by the time they arrived in the Warehouse District of Los Angeles. The roads were dense with traffic. Russell's voice is speaking through the screen's built-in speakers as it sounded muffled, "Alright, you guys are currently in the Warehouse District of the city, there's a white warehouse. You should be able to pull in towards the fence."

"Pull in where?" Darrell questioned.

"It's by your left, you'll be able to open it. It's

abandoned." Darrell stops and turns in between a rusty fence and pulls into a parking area. The area's almost pitch black as there was a shadow blocking the light from the waxing half moon in the obsidian skies. The Lamborghini's headlights illuminate the parking area as it was completely empty with small garages on the other side of the warehouse. "It's awfully small for a meetup," Darrell said.

"I'm bringing the pistol with me," Phoenix said.

"Why?"

"Don't ask, I'm just trying to protect ourselves." The taillights illuminate the entrance of the parking area as Darrell stops the vehicle. He puts the vehicle in park as they get out. They both start walking as they are beside each other. "Good choice to pick talks in negotiation," Darrell said.

"It's dark as hell, I can hardly see." They walk to a faintly white door as they reach the warehouse's sidewalk.

As Darrell opens the door, there is a large, spacious room with dim lights on the ceiling widely separated from each other. Around the warehouse's interior were gray walls with thin support beams widely separated. They look around to study the room as he closes the door behind him. "Now we just have to find where he is," Phoenix said. Darrell looks around to notice a long stairwell ascending onto the edge of a platform. "Let's try up there," he said.

They start walking towards the stairs. The stairwell extended up to twenty-five feet. The wall beside the platform is white in color, but wasn't a bright shade. They noticed a white door on their left.

"It's awfully quiet up here," Darrell said quietly.

"You think?" Phoenix said with her pistol raised in the air. They slow their walking as they approach the door. Phoenix walks towards the door while aiming her pistol towards the ground with both hands. Darrell slowly and cautiously opens the door.

They notice a well-lit hallway as he closes the door behind him. The hallway wasn't big as it was about thirty feet long. They slowly begin walking as they notice an open door on the right side in the middle of the hallway.

They enter through the door noticing a red glow in a medium size room. They see three computers in the center as it was paneled in front of a man sitting by them. He turns around with one of his legs. "Thought you guys wouldn't make it," Russell said.

"Took us almost two days to find you. Brought the vehicle down to almost an empty tank," Darrell said.

"That's what happens when you go on a road trip. Do me a favor and close the door." Darrell takes a couple steps and closes the door. Russell looks at Phoenix ruggedly and blatantly says, "It takes a lot to get down in a city like this."

She gets angry, "You said you were going to explain. I'm giving you a warning, sir. Do *not* waste my time." Russell doesn't crack as he creased his hands, "I can tell that you're wanting something, and I understand that, but there's one thing that you're lacking, miss. It's patience." Phoenix raised her voice and walks a couple steps towards Russell, "First of all, who the hell do you think you are? I've only known you for a couple days and you're already starting to piss me off. And I'm not a person that plays lightly. I want answers and let me make this clear. Don't test my patience."

Russell stands up from his chair and firmly says, "I've only known you for a couple days, too. And I'm noticing that your attitude is getting worse the more I see you. And I'm not the person that plays too lightly with bitches like you. So if you can take a chill pill, you'll be on your merry way."

Russell looks at Phoenix with a frustrated expression, "We'll get along." He quickly snaps his fingers. "Just like that." He raises his eyebrow with a smirk, "Okay?" Phoenix just looks at Russell in disgust as there was a brief pause.

Russell slowly sits back down in his black chair. He turns around to face the computers with his hands behind his head, "So, you guys want to know about the organization?"

"Yes," Darrell said.

"Well, let's go with the basics first. Let's start with the summary of how it all began."

"This should be good," Phoenix said sarcastically. Russell resumed speaking, "It all started in 2017, when Warren Leyton was kidnapped." He turns around and looks at Phoenix, "Does this sound familiar to you, Phoenix?"

"He was my husband," she said. Russell turns around to face the computers to open some kind of database. "He was captured by Barrett Atkinson. He was one of the rookies that worked within the organization. I used to work for them until they took things too far and held themselves against me."

"Yeah, that motherfucker got that bullet inside his sick little head. I did hear from the organization that DNA work was involved." Russell laughs hysterically, thinking it's a joke and turns around, "DNA?!"

Phoenix was getting frustrated, "Yeah? What's so goddamn funny about it? I lost my fucking husband because of him!" Russell was still laughing, but it was calmer, "Are you kidding me? There is no involvement with DNA from the people that work there! That dumbass didn't even know what the hell he was talking about!"

Russell stops laughing, "Barrett only knew how to make up lies just to get somebody in the organization. He was a cheap one, he only knew how to persuade, that bastard."

"Well, everything about the organization is a lie," Darrell said.

"Yeah, you got a point there, but that science talk, that's the funniest shit I've ever heard." Russell turns around to face the computers and types on the keyboard. "Where did you get the computers?" Darrell questioned.

"Long story, it wasn't easy. Things were escalating quickly while you guys were being hunted down."

"We could tell, their vehicles are basically moving weapons now," Darrell said.

"The organization I used to work in was known by the name, the IFHR, short for the International Foundation for

Human Resources." Phoenix was still frustrated as Russell was explaining. "This year marks the thirtieth anniversary of the organization's founding. It was corrupt from the start, at least from when I joined in."

"Well, what did you do to piss them off?" Phoenix questioned.

"I was working in the organization for three years. Everyone started to turn against me in IFHR. Four days before the incident in New York City, I was running towards a door until two of the pricks decided to raise their weapons on me."

"I bet it was easy for you," Darrell said to Russell.

"Yeah, not to mention how fucking big you are," Phoenix said. Russell turned his head around and smiles, "You kidding me?! They had assault rifles, but that didn't fucking bother me! I beat the hell out of them and snapped their necks! Damn rookies."

"Why are you against rookies so much?" Darrell said.

"Rookies are the weakest in the roster, mostly in their

mentality." Phoenix started to get angry as Russell's statement reminded her of Warren. Russell just looked at her, "Hey, he was killed by a rookie." He turns back to face the computers, "But Barrett was right on one thing. They did have a numerical system that applied to everyone within the United States. It was composed of nine digits."

Russell turns towards Darrell, "But since you were chosen to be canceled last time, you decided to run, which made things worse on the organization. Sounds like you guys really pissed them off."

Phoenix said, "Well, no shit. What are you trying to say, Russell?"

"I'm saying that IFHR's building an army." Phoenix gasped and said, "Same thing that Warren said."

"And he was right." Russell turns around again to face the computers, "There are three classes of agents." He counts his fingers while announcing each class, "There's the rookies, the moderates, and the elite agents. Back when you thought you found IFHR's headquarters in New York City, those agents were rookies."

"Wait, how do you know where we've been?" Phoenix questioned.

"The whole organization has been tracking you guys down ever since. While I was attempting to escape, I ran into a control room. I saw both of you on the screen."

"What are you trying to say?" Darrell questioned.

"They're no longer working by numbers, they're taking people by names now."

Darrell and Phoenix look at each other in shock, trying to adjust to the realization of their situation. "What do we do now?" Darrell said.

"We'll talk more about it tomorrow. There will be a place for you guys to stay for the night. I already paid for it."

"Where are we staying?" Phoenix said.

"You're going to be staying at a nearby hotel. It's not far from here. It's right around the corner. And be ready, we're going to meet somewhere else tomorrow, IFHR could be anywhere now. You'll get to meet the mechanic."

"The person you talked to on your communicator?" Darrell said.

"Yes. He's a rookie, but he knows just about as much as I do. Him and I used to work together in the organization. Now get some rest, I have some work to get done."

"Alright, let's go, Phoenix." Phoenix turns around and walks towards the door as they were walking to where they came from. Darrell opened the door as they were walking on the platform in the warehouse's spacious room. "Thought you liked talking to people," said Darrell.

"Not with that guy. Him and I are going to have issues in the future," Phoenix said.

"But now we know more about the organization, we have a name for it, maybe this is becoming a conspiracy, Phoenix." They walk down the stairs to approach ground level and walk to the door.

"Maybe, sometimes I even wonder that myself." Darrell opens the door as they enter outside. He said, "Do you remember when they showed that man that was reported missing in the newspaper last year?" They stop walking and look at each other.

"What are you talking about?" Phoenix questioned.

"I'll explain when we get in the car." They walk to the Lamborghini and open the car doors. They climb into the vehicle as Darrell starts the vehicle and sets it in reverse. He slowly backs out of the parking area and drives on. "He appeared to be of Mexican descent. The caption said that he was interrogated by two men near his front door, white and black in skin color while appearing to be from a business company."

Darrell's words caused Phoenix to think. Suddenly, her eyes widened and she took a slow, and deep breath, "He made me shoot someone in cold blood." She repeated a part of Warren's parting words before he died. "Maybe this is a conspiracy, Darrell."

"They know enough to put that man in a missing persons article, but the media doesn't know about what truly happened. People must not know about our situation, it's not worth getting anybody else involved."

"Then we should stay silent for the night." Darrell looked around the vehicle as he was trying to comprehend what Phoenix was trying to say. He realized she was talking about the broken windows, "Oh, good point."

Darrell stops as he's waiting for a couple vehicles to go. The commuters' vehicles in Los Angeles also comprised of high-priced luxury and high-performance vehicles. Productivity wasn't only present in New York City, but Los Angeles wasn't all that perfect at the time. The crime in the city slowly started to decrease because of the level of prosperity everybody was experiencing. The roads were slightly cleaner as there were few people on the streets that were homeless.

Darrell turns onto another road. The road was dense as it was filled with traffic mostly going the speed limit. He doesn't pay attention to the people around him as he would think that would increase suspicion. He notices a brown four-story building made of bricks. There is a flight of alternating stairs from the second to the fourth floor. It was the Regal Hotel.

Darrell stopped towards an open fence that reveals a parking lot. "Smart man," Darrell said, referring to Russell. He turned right to pull into the parking lot. He sees a large gap by his side for extra parking space. He parked into the gap and shut the vehicle off. "Good choice if you're hiding from an organization," Phoenix said.

Darrell and Phoenix unbuckled their seat belts and got out of the vehicle. They began walking out of the parking lot and towards the hotel. They open the entrance doors to prepare for a night's rest.

Chapter 5: New Ground

July 29, 2020

It was a warm sunny morning as Darrell and Phoenix exit the parking area of Regal Hotel. He turns until he faces the fence.

They notice a small, white auto shop by the side. "Hmm, it wasn't far," he said. He notices that the garage door is fully raised. He saw Russell waving his arm, trying to catch Darrell's attention. "Looks like we're wanted," Phoenix said. Darrell slowly turns and enters the garage.

They entered the garage and exited the vehicle. Phoenix still had her assault rifle behind her back and carried her pistol. They looked around to find Russell, but he wasn't in the room. The garage had windows on one side as they were just below the ceiling, projecting the sun's rays. There are a couple fluorescent light bulbs that extend across the ceiling. The color around the garage's interior projected a tint of sepia, which is a reddish-brown color. While they were still looking around, they saw a steel workstation with several bottles for automobile enhancements and repairs. There were also several types of tools that were arranged by size along with a sink that had smudges of black grease around it.

Darrell and Phoenix walked to a door by the side of the garage. He opens the door to see Russell and the mechanic from his communicator sitting across from each other at a wide, white table. The room they entered in was surrounded by sunlight and was styled like a kitchen. There were white countertops with several wooden cupboards. The floor was hard as it was made of gravel.

Russell looks at Darrell and Phoenix and stands up.

"Wasn't hard to find you," Phoenix said.

"Since you guys are here, we're going to discuss about what it's like in Los Angeles. You're going to have to get used to new ground for a while," Russell said. He looks at them seriously. "This city isn't New York, nothing compared to it. The city's huge, that's for sure, but in a city like this, you really have to watch your back, especially if IFHR's involved." He looks back at the mechanic and says, "You can get up." The mechanic stands up from his chair with a relaxed face. He has a medium build with strong arms. He looked like he visited regularly at a local gym. He was wearing a white tank top with blue denim jeans and gray tennis shoes. He had short blonde hair, almost making him bald. "I'd like you to meet the mechanic. His name's Adrian Wortham. He was one of the top mechanics in the organization. He can fix almost anything." Russell said to Adrian, "Their vehicle took a lot of damage. The windows are pretty much shot along with some dents on the back, but they're small. You may have to see for yourself."

Adrian said to Darrell and Phoenix, "I heard you guys are next on the list. Let's take a look at your vehicle." They walk into the garage to look at the Lamborghini. Russell follows. Adrian was surprised and said, "Damn, how the hell did it get like this?"

"I worked my ass off for this one," Phoenix said. They walked around the Lamborghini as they were inspecting the damage. "Looks like you smuggled one of the elite vehicles. This was never executed by any previous targets before. That's pretty damn impressive," Adrian said as he's looking at the windows. "It definitely needs new glass, that's for sure. What did you use to damage it?"

"A motorcycle. It wasn't an ordinary motorcycle, though."

"Was it silver with a machine gun attached to it?" Phoenix was surprised before she could explain more. "Yes?" she said.

"The motorcycle you operated is mainly used for two-wheeled pursuits. The attachment is a heavily modified gun that is strictly used for military operations. It is portable for a person to hold it with them. Was it manufactured by KTM?" Phoenix shakes her head in confusion, "How do you know all of this?"

"I've been working with vehicles almost all of my life. If you can ask me about any vehicle, I can almost guarantee that I can tell you what it is." Russell looks down on the ground with his arms crossed and looks at Adrian. Darrell and Phoenix do the same thing, looking at Adrian. "Vehicles get special treatment in IFHR, especially for the moderate and elite classed vehicles. Moderate vehicles are similar to elite ones, elites just have more to them, a hell of a lot more. Moderate vehicles have higher privileges than the rookie class. The rookie class is just a group of vehicles with no modifications to them whatsoever. They're vehicles that came out of the factory, to make it short."

Phoenix chuckled and said, "That probably explains why

they were so easy to kill last year." She looks at Darrell, "Took a hard beating from that BMW back there." Darrell glances at Phoenix and returns to looking at Adrian.

Adrian resumes, "But with moderate vehicles, things are different. The vehicles introduced modifications such as performance enhancements, weapon placement, and armory, you just can't see it, it's under the paint. Elite vehicles, however, are the top dogs in the organization's fleet. They're not just higher in performance and weapon capabilities than the moderates, but have a special armor system. I'm pretty sure you guys and Russell have already experienced it."

"The vehicle also had nitrous, too," Darrell said.

"I've been working with the organization for three years to know enough and remember what happened."

"Wait, what happened?" Darrell said.

"This only happened about a week ago." Darrell and Phoenix look at each other in surprise. Adrian begins to explain his side of the story as they attempt to visualize it. "I was working with the moderate vehicles in one of the organization's holding units. It was huge, too. It could fit about two hundred vehicles at one time. I was working on a yellow Ferrari, wondering why the hell I got into the organization in the first place." Adrian looks down to think. He lifts his head back up as he starts to get nervous, "The next thing I know, a loud alarm starts going off. Agents were running from all directions. They were running towards the nearest vehicle they could get their hands on. As they started their engines, the garage door was covering an entire wall. I covered my eyes because of the bright skies from outside. Everybody started flooring it as they exited out of the holding unit."

Darrell and Phoenix were surprised as they followed along with Adrian's vision. "What happened with you and Russell?" Darrell questioned.

"The next thing I knew was that Russell was running towards the vehicle I was at, which was an indigo Nissan. He said, 'We have to go!' So, we rushed into the vehicle and drove ourselves out of there, but the moderates and the elites weren't the only ones operating by the time." Phoenix and Darrell were shocked. "By the time we got out of there, there were also militant vehicles of different kinds."

Phoenix tensed up, "What kind of militant vehicles?"

Russell says, "Let's just say they're bigger and stronger than the elites." Adrian glances at Russell and looks back at Darrell and Phoenix. "We have to step up our game this time. You can stay here for now. Later, I'll discuss the first mission for heading out tomorrow," Russell said.

"Missions? We don't do missions," Phoenix questioned.

"Do you guys want to know why the organization is after you or not, Phoenix?" She looks at Russell, frustrated. She sighs and gives in, "Fine."

"Alright, but for right now, Adrian will be helping you with your vehicle. You guys are going to have to get out of the garage."

Darrell and Phoenix walk into the kitchen along with Russell while Adrian prepares to work on the Lamborghini. They walk upstairs as they are following Russell. "This place was also abandoned, too," Russell said. "But we had no choice but to make this our home." While they were walking upstairs, they notice a room that was about fifty feet long. The room had wood-stained walls. There were a couple windows by a computer setup, but were high enough to where people from the outside world couldn't see inside. The computer setup was similar to the one back at the abandoned warehouse. The computers were on top of a light brown desk that extended almost to the entire room. "This looks familiar," Phoenix said.

"I moved the computer set up from the warehouse," Russell said. Phoenix looked at him in disbelief. Russell looks at her and said, "My car's a four-seater." He sits down in a brown office chair in front of the computers and moves his mouse around to wake it up. "The organization doesn't only hide in one spot. They're not only working in New York City anymore."

"So what's the situation?" Darrell questioned.

"IFHR's going to a national level now. They've been planning this ever since you were picked." Russell opens up the database of IFHR with its insignia on the computer screen. The screen turned black as it showed a map zooming out of the screen, projecting the United States. "Our first target won't be located in this area. We're going to go out of state for this." Darrell and Phoenix walk up to the computer screen.

While the computer screen is trying to detect a possible link to the organization, the map zoomed into an area outside of California. It zoomed into the state of Michigan. The screen shows a picture of a man that has short black hair, blue eyes, and is white in skin color. Russell says, "Our first mission is going to be hiding out in Detroit, Michigan. His name is Arden Kendrick. Twenty-five years of age. One-hundred and seventy pounds. He was just enrolled into the organization about a year back."

"What does he do?" Phoenix said.

"He has two main objectives. To gain intel on other possible targets and of course, track you guys down."

"Is there anything we need to watch out for?" Darrell said.

"Yes, he's a wheelman. He may be a rookie, but he sure knows how to get the hell out of a situation. He also can move around the environment pretty well, he's into parkour. He drives a midnight blue Audi. It's a discontinued model, its year of production was in 2008."

"Just tell us what we need to do before I get pissed off," Phoenix said impatiently.

"Hmm, touché," Russell said blatantly. Phoenix got angry. "You guys are going to have to get some sleep. You may want to check on your vehicle."

After a couple hours of passing, Darrell and Phoenix walked out of the room and downstairs into the kitchen. After they opened the door, they saw Adrian still working on the

Lamborghini in the garage. There was a black platform that

suspended the vehicle to about five feet. It is also supported

by a jack.

They walked towards the vehicle when they saw Adrian

working under the chassis. He had small black grease marks

on his face. "How's the vehicle?" Darrell questioned.

"Performance is still intact, weapons are still plentiful,

mirrors are fixed, just a few other minor fixes that need to be

applied. I changed the oil for you guys, it was starting to

become brown. Honey-yellow oil is sufficient for better

performance," Adrian said.

"What about the windows and the armor?" Phoenix said.

"I'll work on that later. This may take me all night before

you guys take off on the road."

"We already have our first mission," Darrell said. Phoenix

said, "Somebody named Arden Kendrick. It didn't surprise us

about what the mission's goal was."

"Nothing really surprises me anymore. You've been wanted since the start of your pursuit. Everybody knows about you guys in the organization," Adrian said. He looks at them, "And don't mind Russell. He talks like that most of the time I'm around him."

"You don't say," Phoenix said while raising her eyebrow.

"He can be an asshole sometimes. I'm used to it, but he can be crazy, though."

"Why would you say crazy?"

"While him and I were working in the organization, he always talked about getting out of the place and escaping. I told him he was insane if he tried even with the littlest effort. But apparently it worked, he does get stubborn sometimes. Just wanted to let you guys know about that." Adrian walks away from the vehicle to wash the grease off of his hands and face. "Because in today's society, the world can be a dangerous place." He splashes cold water on his face from the running faucet. He takes a white towel sitting by the edge of the sink to dry his face off and sighs, "Alright, guys. I'm going to take a break for right now. I'll try to get done with your vehicle by tonight."

"Alright," Phoenix said.

Before Darrell and Phoenix go back in the kitchen, Adrian wanted to say more, "Oh, and one more thing, guys. I would be careful for when you go out there."

"What are you trying to say?" Darrell questioned.

"I'm trying to keep you guys out of trouble."

"What do you mean trouble, what could go wrong, Adrian?" Phoenix said.

"Today's economy may be prosperous, but you guys may be the start of a conspiracy one day. I'll talk about this later. I have to get some work done."

"Alright, we'll be upstairs. We have to improvise a plan for tomorrow's mission," Phoenix said.

"Okay, I'll let you know what's up. Here's another word of advice for today."

"What's that?" Phoenix said.

"Set up contacts. We're going to have to keep in touch as much as possible while this is happening."

Darrell and Phoenix close the door and sit at the table across from each other in the kitchen. Phoenix firmly looks at Darrell and whispers, "I'm not too sure about this, Darrell."

"What do you mean?" he whispered.

"From what Adrian said, maybe this is the start of a conspiracy." They pull out their cell phones and exchange phone numbers. "We can't say anything to Russell. We need to keep this between us and Adrian," Phoenix said. Darrell hesitates and looks at Phoenix, "Okay."

"Let's go back upstairs. He probably wants us up there."

Darrell and Phoenix get up from the table and walk upstairs. Russell is still sitting in front of the computers. He turns around and says, "So, how's the vehicle?"

"Got an oil change, it just needs to be fixed with the armor and the windows, of course," Darrell said.

"So, what's the plan?" Phoenix questioned. Russell looks at the computer screens and says, "First off, you're going to have to leave early tomorrow. While you're down there, you're going to need communication."

Russell gets up and walks to a black steel filing cabinet with three sliders. Darrell and Phoenix follow him. He opens the middle cabinet to reveal several communication devices arranged in a neat order. The devices are slightly more advanced in technology than in their present time. He grabbed a couple microphones, which were small attachments to the ears and are chrome in color. He set the microphones on top of the filing cabinet. He then grabbed a couple communicators that were perfectly circular in shape. They were about the size of a little over half of his hand. They had a black glossy finish to them.

Russell walks up to Darrell and Phoenix with the microphones and communicators and said, "Alright, this is just a slew of the telecommunication network in IFHR." He sets down the microphones and one of the communicators by the computers. He lets out the communicator and shows them how to use it while pointing at certain parts, "This communicator has two different functions. This model would be considered the basic level of entry during operations within the organization. Telecommunications within the organization are used mostly during espionage and hit missions." Russell points to the top of the communicator with a couple buttons, "These are the two functions of the basic model, they are COMM and MIC. COMM is optional for certain operations, but mostly if you're far away from your target. COMM is a little bit risky because if you use that function, you have to speak directly into the communicator in order for the sender to connect to the person receiving it. You'll have a higher chance of getting compromised during a mission if you're not careful enough. I would recommend using MIC for any operation. Using MIC eliminates the purpose of COMM. With MIC, you have a better chance of succeeding in an operation."

"So, I'm taking that we shouldn't bother with COMM?" Phoenix said.

"Yes, however, the communicator still has to be used in order to communicate solely through the microphone. There's a button on the side that you have to hold in order to speak and send a message. Sound won't pick up if you don't hold it. Once you completed your message, release the button. Think of it like a walkie-talkie."

Russell sets the communicator by the computer desk with the rest of the equipment, "Now, I'm assuming that you guys want to know where you can sleep for the night?"

"Yes, where would that be?" Phoenix said.

"Follow me." Russell walks out of the room as Darrell and Phoenix follow him. They walk downstairs and into the kitchen. While looking around, there is a hallway that was located on the opposite side of the garage. They walk into the hallway to see a couple doors on one side. Russell points out each of the doors by their room, "This is the bathroom." After pointing out the bathroom, there were two other doors beside it. "The other doors lead to a living room and a bedroom. You guys will be sleeping in the living room tonight." Phoenix looks around and notices a crack that's about the size of a door by the bedroom. "What's that?" Phoenix said. Russell looks in the direction of Phoenix, "I don't know. That's actually been there by the time we first got here."

As Russell opens the living room door, the doors reveal a medium-sized space that has an olive green carpet and burnt-sienna stained walls, a reddish-brown color. The room was being lit up by a couple white fluorescent tubes from the ceiling. There are no windows in the room. There were two recliners and two couches separated from both sides. Beside the recliners and couches are lamps with one beside each of them. "What do you guys think?" Russell said.

"Looks comfortable," Darrell said. Phoenix slowly nodded her head, but didn't express impression.

"Might want to get comfortable for later. You guys need as much sleep as you can. There'll be blankets behind the recliners for when you guys get cold. You shouldn't worry about that too much since this is technically a warehouse. You'll be locked in from the outside world for a little while."

"It looks better that way," Phoenix said.

Several hours later, the day turns into night. Only the lamps were on at this time. Darrell and Phoenix are in the living room as they're both pulling blankets stacked on each other by the door. Phoenix set her pistol and assault rifle by the door. They both walk to the recliners with their blankets and sit next to each other. They press a button on the side of the recliners to extend them, making themselves comfortable. They pull the blankets over top of them as they are laying back. "A lot has changed," Phoenix said. Darrell turns his head to face Phoenix and said, "What do you mean?"

"Look at the world around us. It's changing in our eyes."

"What's happening to you?" Darrell said confusingly.

Phoenix looks at Darrell, "You mean what's happening to us? Maybe Adrian is right. Maybe we are the start of a conspiracy." Darrell takes a sigh. "We can't let Russell know about our situation."

"What do you have against Russell so much?"

"I just don't like the guy. I'm not fond with the employees of a corrupt organization."

"We should probably get some rest," Darrell said.

"We should, can't keep complaining about society now. Won't get us anywhere. We already know how fucked up it is."

Darrell and Phoenix turn off their lamps and prepare themselves for sleep, awaiting departure for their first mission.

Chapter 6: Rave

August 1, 2020

Detroit, Michigan

It is nighttime as Darrell and Phoenix cruise on a busy

road in the center of Detroit. The infrastructure of the city

was well lit. The obsidian skies were clear as the waxing

three-quarters moon was present. The buildings were

massive as they varied in several shapes and sizes with their

updated, modern architecture.

There were still small dents around the Lamborghini

from the vehicular confrontation. Darrell turns to the right to

follow the directions of where Russell pinpointed. Russell's

voice is slightly muffled through the Lamborghini's

communication system, "Alright, now you're going to see a large building about twenty stories high."

"There's the Audi," Phoenix whispered. Russell continued, "Drive past that building until you make a left, you're going to park in an alleyway beside it. There won't be anybody that will notice you. There are no residential buildings around it. Just a small light towards the end of the alleyway."

Darrell stops and turns as they're on a road that's overcast by the shadows of the buildings beside it. The only sources of light were the street lamps and the faint window illuminations on both sides of the street. Darrell stops and slowly turns into the alleyway. Upon entering, there was a light protruding about eight feet from the ground with a mounted security camera by its side. "We're here," Darrell said.

"Alright, now when you guys get out of the car, I want you to go into the front entrance of the building. You need to blend in with the crowd in order to avoid suspicion and pull

this off successfully," Russell said.

"What's in the building?" Phoenix said.

"The place is a dance club. It's going to be awfully busy

tonight. It might be a tight squeeze, but use the environment

around you to your advantage. It would be a good idea to get

out now."

"Alright," Darrell said.

Right before they get out of the car, Russell forget to tell

them something, except he was talking to them through their

communicators. "Oh, and I almost forgot, there are two

yellow tickets in the glove box. Take those with you. There will

be two bouncers in security uniform standing by the entrance

to take your tickets," he said.

Phoenix opens the glove box and pulls the tickets out

and places them in her pocket. They get out of the vehicle

and walk out of the alleyway. They are walking beside each

other. "Since we're out of the vehicle, we can talk about the situation," Phoenix said firmly.

"What?" Darrell said.

"We both know that Russell and Adrian used to work for IFHR, but I don't think I trust one of them."

"You're talking about Russell, are you?"

"I don't really trust the guy, he sometimes tries to distance himself, have you noticed that?"

"Yeah, but he may be trying to help us, same with Adrian." They both walk on the sidewalk of the street.

"Like I said, Darrell, I don't play around with agents."

"It can't be that bad, they said they used to work for them."

"But what I'm trying to say is that at least Adrian is more willing to help us out. I'm going to be cautious and watch my back, no matter what the circumstances are. In a world like this, you can't really trust anyone."

They walk to the right and notice the two bouncers from the distance by the front entrance. "That's our way in,"

Phoenix said. They continued to walk until they reached the front entrance. The front entrance is made of glass doors. The bouncers have a large build, bald and are white in skin color. They are both wearing black shades of sunglasses. Their uniforms are all in black as they looked like a police officer at first glance. They were wearing a patch that showed the insignia of the Detroit Police Department. The patches had a yellow outline. They have a portable radio clipped onto their side. That's when they realized they were police officers. One of the officers take their hand out, "Tickets please." Phoenix takes the tickets out and shows them to the officers, "Got these in advance."

The other officer inspects the tickets and looks at Darrell and Phoenix. Instead of taking the tickets, he lifts his thumb and moves it behind him, signaling that their admission is accepted. "Thank you," Phoenix said.

The officers open the doors for them. They walk into a small hallway that's decorated with a welcoming atmosphere.

The walls and the floor are the color of burnt orange as they were on a rug that's beige.

As Darrell and Phoenix exit the hallway, they notice a room that was emitting a large amount of thin rays of sky blue lights. They looked around to see the room filled with people dancing to the loud electronic music played throughout the room's surround system. They looked straight to see a large screen projecting a visualization fluctuating to the music's rhythm. In front of the visualization was a disk jockey standing on a stage in front of expensive equipment specifically for music production and mixing software. He was wearing headphones and was raising his fist as he was enthusiastic with the rhythm. Russell speaks through the communicator, "You guys in the club?" Darrell holds MIC and responds, "Yes." He releases the button.

"Surprised about the venue?"

"Nothing surprises me much anymore," Phoenix said. Russell says, "It's easy to blend in. Each person is like a ghost in a place like this. People can do anything in a rave club, but don't get too comfortable now. And don't get lost in the crowd. The target could be anywhere. Keep a watchful eye out for Arden. Try to find an open place to where you can see almost the whole environment around you. And pretend that you're part of the crowd until you see the target." The connection was dismissed.

"But, why would he choose a rave club?" Phoenix said in a confused manner.

Darrell and Phoenix look around to find an open spot on the dance floor. "Let's go in the center," Darrell said. He lets his hand out to Phoenix. She was hesitant and raised her eyebrow. "Come on, you'll be safe with me." Phoenix looks around and tries to comprehend with what Darrell is trying to say. She widens her eyes, "Oh, okay. Didn't know what you were trying to say for a minute." She puts on an elated smile, feigning her emotions.

Darrell and Phoenix both lock hands as they walk to the

center of the dance floor. "Don't worry, I'll watch. I got you,"

Darrell said. Phoenix smiles flirtatiously, "We'll just blend right

in." He's looking at the stage. They both extend their arms

and placed them on each other's shoulders. They start

dancing as they're moving their hips. They both smile as

they're acting like they're having a good time. "There's a lot in

this place. So many people," Darrell said.

"I'm not the negotiable type. Not really much of a talker

anymore."

"Hey, your secret's safe with me. Nobody has to know

about it as long as I'm here."

Darrell peered his head to the right. He notices the man

that matched the same features from Russell's briefing

standing by a guardrail. He wore the same business attire for

IFHR. "I think that's him," Darrell said. Phoenix was caught off

guard. They stopped dancing and let go of each other. "What?

You see somebody that you know?" Phoenix said.

"Yeah, it's a long-lost friend. You might recognize him,

too."

"Well, let's go see him." They slowly walk out of the center as they gently squeeze through the people dancing. As they walk off of the dance floor, they hold hands. They walk to Arden. "Hey, Arden!" Phoenix yelled. Arden was startled. He notices that Darrell and Phoenix are sprinting towards him. They stop sprinting as they are about a half of a foot away from him. "Hey, buddy, how've you been?" Phoenix said sarcastically. Arden was confused, "Who are you guys?"

"We're the ones that are going to kick your ass," Darrell boldly said.

"Does this ring a bell?" Phoenix takes her communicator out and shows it to Arden. He was hesitant for a moment. "Shit!" Arden panicked. He attempted to barge through Darrell and Phoenix, but grab a hold of him. Arden was struggling as they still managed to maintain their grip on his arms, "Oh, no, you're not going anywhere," Darrell said.

"Until we get our answers," Phoenix said.

Arden gets angry and headbutts Darrell. He kicks him in the knee a couple times until Darrell loses his grip. He performs a hard left hook at Darrell, causing him to grunt and almost hit the floor. Arden now puts his focus on Phoenix. Phoenix had a determined look as she's still holding on to Arden. She attempts to move behind him and grab his other arm. Arden swung his body around, which caught her off guard. He violently pushes Phoenix up against the guardrail. She attempts to charge at Arden, "You motherfu-" Arden swings his arm and performs a hard right hook, causing her to grunt and thud to the floor. Darrell attempts to charge at Arden, but he punches Darrell straight in his face, almost giving him a bloody nose.

Arden sprints towards the front entrance doors and pushes them anxiously as he was hyperventilating. He alerted the officers as he ran towards his car. "Hey, where the hell do you think you're going?! The party's not over yet!" One of the officers said. Arden ignores them. "HEY! Get the fuck back here!" The officers start running after Arden as he enters his

Audi. He starts the car and speeds away from the dance club. The officers pull out their semi-automatic pistols and shoot at the vehicle. They run out of bullets by the time Arden was out of their sight.

Darrell helps Phoenix stand by pulling her arm up. She was enraged, "I'm going to get that fucking bastard!" Russell speaks, "Hey, what the fuck are you guys doing? Don't let him get away!" Darrell looks around to find the back door of the building, which is covered with a thick shadow, but still visible. "This way, our vehicle should still be back there! Come on!" Darrell said.

They start running towards the back door. They budge through it as they sprint through a small, bland hallway made of concrete as it was lit by a sepia-tinted light throughout it. They budge through another door as it leads to outside. They run down the small steps to get to the Lamborghini. They quickly get into the car as Phoenix grabs her pistol and cocks it. "That son of a bitch just dug his own grave," she said.

"Guys, hurry! He's about five hundred feet away from you. He may be turning left in a few seconds!" Russell said.

Darrell sets the vehicle in reverse and floors the throttle until he turns the steering wheel hard at the end of the alleyway. He straightens the vehicle and sets it into drive. Darrell and Phoenix are now engaged in hot pursuit of the target.

Chapter 7: Deception

"Guys, step on it!" Russell said.

"Russell, shut the fuck up!" Phoenix yelled. Darrell

shifted into second gear. He was slightly gaining distance as

he started to hear the tumult of the Audi's engine. Arden

drifted to the left into a road with buildings on both sides.

As Darrell drifts, Phoenix rolls down the window and

takes her pistol. "Just like the good old days," she said boldly.

She aims the pistol at the Audi's tires. Arden quickly drifts to

the far left side of the road as Darrell immediately follows

him. She puts both of her hands on the trigger and fires at the tires. It takes a couple shots each to bust them.

Arden pressed on the brakes to prevent collision. "Shit!" he panicked. He stopped by an alleyway.

"Darrell, stop the car!" Phoenix said. The Lamborghini's tires screeched to a complete stop as it was right beside Arden's. Arden starts running into the alleyway. "Get out of the car, chase after him!" Russell said.

They get out and start running into the alleyway. As they enter the dark shadows of it, Arden runs up a flight of steps that's about five feet high. He starts wall running and jumps down to the ground to exit the flight of steps. Phoenix taunted Arden, "What's the matter, Arden?! Can't take your deception?" Darrell ran up the steps, but doesn't wall run. They jump over the guardrail and towards the ground to resume the foot pursuit. Phoenix fires a shot at Arden, but barely misses. Arden begins running to the right and starts wall running again. He ends the wall run by jumping to the other side and grabbing a hold of a platformed stairwell. He dangled from the ground as he was suspended ten feet in the air. His body was being lit up by a blue neon light above it.

Darrell and Phoenix stopped running as they saw Arden. Phoenix slowly walks toward Arden as she's lifting her pistol to aim at him. Arden panics. Phoenix applies more force on the trigger and fires a round at Arden's hand. The bullet immediately pierced through Arden's finger, cutting it clean off and making him scream in agonizing pain. The bullet also caused the metal of the platform to slightly bend. Arden lets go of the stairwell and fell to the ground on his back. He is grunting from his severed finger. Arden can barely move now.

They run up to Arden and start punching and kicking him. He started screaming again from the additional pain. "Stop, please! I'll tell you!" Arden begs. They stop beating him, but Phoenix wasn't finished. She quickly crouched down and grabs him by the neck. Phoenix was infuriated, "So, go ahead, tell me. Why did you pick him?"

"Pick who?!" Arden yelled. Phoenix tightened her grip on

Arden's neck, "You know damn well who I'm talking about!"

"Phoenix, stop!" Darrell walked up to Phoenix, trying to intervene, but Phoenix wouldn't budge. She snapped at Darrell, "WHAT?! I thought you wanted answers, too! Apparently you don't fully know how I feel about the situation!" Darrell raises his arms and steps back from Phoenix. She points the gun at Arden's forehead. Arden starts laughing heartlessly, "You're going to kill me anyway, aren't you?"

"You better give me the damn answers before you really test my patience!" Phoenix threatens.

"Alright." Arden takes a deep breath as Phoenix is trembling with emotions. "I'm just here to kill you and that's my only mission." Phoenix was growing impatient. She takes the pistol and violently bashes Arden's head with it, "Why did you choose Warren?!" Arden's face started to get bloodied and bruised from the impacts. "Because that's we do, Phoenix. We're just the start of it. I'm a rookie. There's way more than a fleet of vehicles. There's a whole lot more to it

and you better be ready because we're coming for you,"

Arden said.

Phoenix started to become calmer, "I see how it is now.

With every person working in your fucking sickhouse, you're

just as stubborn as everyone else I've placed a bullet in."

"So, why don't you kill me now? Make it worse for

yourself."

Phoenix stands up and keeps her aim at Arden's

forehead, "I'm not making it worse for myself, I'm doing

something for someone I lost because of you." Arden doesn't

show any emotion. "And if anybody's not able to get back

with you, THEY better be ready!" Phoenix cocks the gun,

"Because I'm Phoenix Leyton." Arden widened his eyes,

petrified. "And he was my husband." Arden let his trembling

arm out with his severed finger. "NOOOOOOO!"

Phoenix shot a round at Arden's forehead, jolting his

head back, killing him instantly. Phoenix was angrily breathing heavily. Darrell was in shock from what just happened.

"Phoenix, what the hell is wrong with you?!" he yelled. She shows no remorse. He uses his communicator, "Russell!"

"What? What's the matter, did you get him?" Darrell sighs, "Yes, we got him." He looks at Phoenix angrily. "He wasn't killed, was he?!" Russell yelled. There was a moment of hesitation. Darrell heard Russell take a heavy sigh and yelled, "Goddamnit! You were supposed to get him alive!"

Phoenix said, "Why? He wasn't good at explaining things. Didn't have the nerve to do it."

"But did you at least get some answers?!" There was a slight hesitation. Darrell said, "We did get some answers, apparently, we're dealing with more than just a fleet of vehicles chasing after us."

"Alright, we'll discuss this more when you get back to Los Angeles. Get out of Detroit as soon as you can before an agent discovers you guys by Arden. They keep track of who dies. Like I said, they keep a database now."

"We'll see you back at L.A.," Darrell releases the button on the communicator. He and Phoenix begin walking in the dark part of the alleyway to get to their vehicle.

They give each other frustrated looks while climbing into the vehicle. Darrell starts the car and drives away from the alleyway. He turned left and looked at Phoenix, "What's going on with you, Phoenix?"

"Never felt so good to get revenge," Phoenix said.

"Okay, you know what? He could've given us answers. We could've known what else is after us."

"How would you know that? He only knew deception, Darrell. He's just like the rest of them. Trying to keep their secrets."

Chapter 8: Preparation

August 3, 2020

Downtown Los Angeles, California

The sun brightens the city on a Monday morning as

Darrell pulls into the abandoned auto shop. Adrian looked

behind him while he was arranging his tools in his toolbox.

They get out of the vehicle and walk to the kitchen door.

Phoenix was holding her pistol along with her assault rifle

hoisted behind her back. Darrell and Phoenix are still

frustrated. "No damage," Darrell said. Adrian stared at the

door and he sighed. After the door closed, he turned around

and resumed what he was doing.

They walk upstairs to the computer room. Russell was

sitting in front of the screens as he saw them coming his way.

"So, what's the situation?" Russell said.

"Well, he wasn't a wheelman, pursuit only lasted for about a minute," Darrell said.

"What else happened?"

Phoenix said, "Well, I shot the bastard's finger off. Wasn't much of a talker, though."

"It was like you guys said before, we have to watch out for more than what we think is going on," Darrell said.

"Yes, Arden was right on that part." Russell began typing to bring up the map and database. "What are you doing?" Phoenix said.

"Bringing up the next possible mission for the answers you're looking for," Russell said. He zooms the map into a couple states to the right just above California. "It looks like your next mission will be hiding out in Yellowstone."

"Which state?" Darrell said.

"You mean what states? The national park's main state is

Wyoming, but it also extends into Montana and Idaho."

"What's happening in Yellowstone?" Phoenix said.

"Well, the mission will be hiding in the park area located in Montana," Russell said. He opens up the database on the right side of the screen. He viewed not just the names of every agent affiliated in IFHR, but also every base and stronghold that has been constructed since its establishment. They walk up to Russell to see a building appearing to be composed of stainless steel. "There's a secret military weapons base that's in the center of the state's park area. It was put there for a reason, so that way no one would ever be able to know about it or get through it." Phoenix raises her eyebrow in disbelief. "But here's the thing, though, know how the organization's supposed to be kept a secret?"

"Yeah?" What about it?" Phoenix said.

"These computers are only accessible to the elite class, which means that you have every piece of information that the organization has ever created in its growing database of archives. Took me a hell of a time to snatch these damn computers." Russell sighs, "Elites are fucking crazy."

"So, what's so special about the base?" Darrell said.

"Like I said, with these types of computers, you have access to every piece of information from every agent, base, and all of the other things happening throughout the organization."

"So, what are you trying to tell us, Russell?" Phoenix said.

"They're stupid enough to log their fucking passcode of every base."

"Well, this should be easy," she said. Russell points his finger up, "But don't get too ahead of yourself, they still have an obsession with numbers." He clicked on the picture of the base and said, "Look at the length of the passcode." Darrell and Phoenix lean forward to examine it. Each passcode is twenty numbers long. "Damn," Darrell said. "That's more than my workplace. Even that's complicated enough."

Russell moves the mouse arrow to the database to click

on the weapons base. It also revealed the massive list of agents currently working there. He clicks on one of the agents' names to reveal the portrait of a man that's white in skin color and has the same head shape as Russell. He is bald and has a tough look on his face and also has blue eyes. Russell reads the agent's profile, "Conway Barkevich. Age, 31. 185 pounds. He's been working for the organization for two years starting today. He recently graduated to a moderate level, giving him exposure and privileges to work with entry-level modified weapons such as the pistol you're holding, Phoenix." She looks down on her pistol. "Let me see your pistol," Russell interrupted.

Phoenix gives Russell her pistol. He turned it around to study its shape and model. He looked at the size of the gun's barrel to determine its type. He sets the gun down by the keyboard. Russell starts explaining about the gun, "The gun that you're holding, is one of the most secretive weapons in the organization. A weapon like that can pierce right through a person with just one bullet. The organization didn't start making modified prototypes until 2014. They have a tendency to use technology to its advantage. Because of the types of equipment and tactics that IFHR has at its disposal, they'll keep advancing in order to stay one step ahead of their game." Russell gives back her pistol.

"So, what do we do now?" Darrell said.

"We prepare, of course. I'm going to come with you guys on this one. So, that means I have to get out my business attire." Russell stands up and walks towards the filing cabinet. He pulls open the top drawer to reveal a black suit jacket, tie, pants, shoes, and white dress shirt. "I also have extra clothes for you guys. They're different than my outfit."

Russell crouches down and pulls the bottom drawer to reveal two outfits all in black. He pulls them out to reveal that they are mostly denim. They're suspended by a chrome metal hanger. It is a jacket with pockets on the inside and outside, jeans, black shades of sunglasses, and hiking boots. Phoenix asks, "Why would we need hiking boots?"

"Because we're going into the wilderness. You're also going to need extra weapons in your personal arsenal specifically for this mission." Russell sets the clothes down by the computer desk. "I'll be right back. Stay right here, I'll be back in a few minutes." He walks towards the door and goes downstairs. Phoenix whispers, "Wonder why he wants us to stay here."

"I don't know," Darrell whispers.

After a couple minutes have passed, Darrell and Phoenix were startled by a loud clang from the kitchen. Darrell said, "What the hell was that?" Phoenix readies her pistol and takes precaution, "You know that crack in the wall by Russell's bedroom? That door could lead to somewhere. One of these days, we may have to go behind that door."

They can hear Russell coming up the stairs from his loud footsteps. He walks towards the computer room with several cutting tools in his hands. He set the tools down by the computer desk to carefully arrange them. They walk to

Russell as he's sorting them out. "These are daggers and knives," Russell said. The daggers are black and are sharp enough to cut through other metallic surfaces. Darrell and Phoenix noticed two other objects that are black in color. They are about the size of a large candy bar for the handle. "What are those?" Darrell said.

"These are the knives, Darrell," Russell answered. He picks one of them up to demonstrate its features. There are two buttons on the handle of the knife. One on the front and back. He presses both buttons as two silver curved blades quickly come out of the main blade. Darrell and Phoenix were shocked. "Damn," Darrell said.

"And then the front button just extends the regular blade like you see with other knives." Russell presses both of the buttons again to close the blades. He picks up a dagger to demonstrate them. They are the shape of arrowheads and had a small black handle on the bottom of them. "For the daggers, both of you will have a set of five to use. These daggers were carefully crafted with obsidian as well as carbon. The carbon was crafted to cut through materials that are as hard as red mahogany, one of the strongest types of wood." Russell moves the dagger away from himself. "These are also lightweight, too. These will inflict damage from at least seventy-five feet away." He sets down the daggers by the knives. Darrell and Phoenix walk to the assortment of knives and daggers. "I would get a good night's rest if I were you, things may get a little blusterous tomorrow."

"Why do you say that?" Phoenix said.

"There's going to be military vehicles there. We need to stay on top of our game in order to pull this off." They hesitate as they look at each other.

After Darrell and Phoenix are done checking out the assortment, they walk downstairs as Russell resumes working in front of the computers. They walk into the kitchen and into the hallway of the living room. Phoenix points out the door-sized crack by Russell's bedroom, "That's the door I was talking about, Darrell." Darrell just looks at the door, "What do you think it could be?"

"Don't know, but it looks like they're definitely hiding something." Phoenix firmly looks at him. "We can't let Adrian know either. I don't trust him either, but he seems like a decent guy."

"Oh, *now* you think that someone's decent?" Darrell said. Phoenix raises her eyebrow in frustration. They walk towards the garage. Darrell opens the door to see that Adrian is working on the Lamborghini's bodywork to remove most of its dents. Adrian looked at them, "Oh, hey, guys."

"Hey," Phoenix said.

"How are you?"

"Good, how are you?" Darrell said. Adrian stops working on the car, "Good, what's your next mission?"

"Yellowstone," Phoenix said. "Russell's coming with us." Adrian hesitates and gives out a sigh, "Why does he want to come with you?" Phoenix said, "We're assuming that we can't do it alone. He said that there's going to be military vehicles by the base we're heading to." Adrian looks down in frustration. "What's wrong, Adrian?" Darrell said.

"Russell can be a nut sometimes, sometimes good, sometimes bad. If you push him too much, he'll get pissed off in no time. He can be unpredictable at times. I'm warning you guys, that's how I'm trying to help you."

Adrian heard Russell's footsteps as Darrell and Phoenix were startled. Russell slowly opens the door and says, "Hey, how are you guys doing?"

"We're doing good," Phoenix said. "We're discussing about the mission." Russell looks down and says, "Oh." He hesitates and looks back up, "Is everything alright?"

"Yeah, we're fine," Darrell said.

"Okay, let me know if there's something wrong, alright?"

"Okay," Phoenix said. Russell closes the door and walks back upstairs. Adrian smiles and says, "I can help you guys."

"Since when do you come in?" Phoenix said, raising her

eyebrow.

"I can help you get some skilled driving in your genes." Darrell and Phoenix just look at him. Adrian raises his arms and widens his eyes, "What? I'm a mechanic. I do this for a living!" Darrell and Phoenix laugh. Phoenix said, "So, what do you have in mind?"

"Well, Russell doesn't know about it. It will be in an unincorporated town in California. There used to be an established destination of IFHR there." Darrell and Phoenix look at each other. "Well, let's hope you know what you're doing, Adrian. That's all I have to say," Phoenix said.

"The base was only abandoned for about a couple months, there should be no people there. We shouldn't have any problem getting in."

"What's around the base?"

"Outside the base is a network of winding roads, a section with a range of man-made geographical settings, and an extensive indoor training course used for a range of several possible emergency scenarios. I'll discuss more tomorrow. I'm pretty sure that Russell wants you to get some rest tonight."

"I'm not too sure about this, Adrian. Russell might find out about this," Darrell said.

"I may have to tell him where we're going, he might even tag along, too. Perhaps he might've already planned it." Darrell and Phoenix walk out of the garage and into the kitchen and into the computer room. "What are you guys up to?" Russell said.

"Just got done talking to Adrian about the mission," Phoenix said.

"Oh, I almost forgot, there's an abandoned base in California. It has a training course that's set up for several possible scenarios."

"Why would we need a training course? I already have a stuntman as a partner." Russell looks at them and raises his eyebrow, "Darrell, how good are you with off-road?" Darrell couldn't think of what to say, "Ugh."

"Exactly." Russell turned to face the computer again. "The base will have a set of geographical features for certain environments. I may get Adrian to tag along with us." Phoenix and Darrell were hesitant. "What? He's also a good instructor when it comes to driving, since he's a mechanic. I'll guide you through the weapons and tactical stages of the training course. I would get some rest if I were you. It may take a couple days before we can meet in Montana."

Later on at night, Darrell and Phoenix are in the living room while setting up for bed after getting cleaned up. Meanwhile, Russell is in the bathroom, standing in front of a mirror. The bathroom was rather small in size as the walls were white. There was a shower cabinet with a gray curtain behind Russell. He slowly took off his shirt to reveal his stocky, muscular body. He grabbed the black electric razor on the sink and started shaving his hair. He slowly made it to the back of his skull. He kept shaving until there was no hair left on his scalp. Once he was done, he looked himself in the

mirror, filled with anger and pride. He matched the same

features of Conway Barkevich. Like a wolf in sheep's wool,

blending in the organization will be their next challenge.

Chapter 9: Training

August 4, 2020

New Idria, California

Darrell, Phoenix, Russell, and Adrian are traveling together on a sunny day at noon. Adrian's vehicle is a white high-performance model from Audi as it was in a moderate class. Darrell and Russell are driving beside each other as Adrian was behind them. They were driving on a submerged stretch of land as it was about three hundred feet above the ground. There were bushes scattered as there was barely any trace of grass. "Okay, now what you're going to do is turn right, we'll enter into New Idria there," Russell said over the communication system.

They all turn to see a couple buildings that are battered and aged from the town's desertion. They're now driving on mixed road that's made of dirt and gravel. "Okay, guys, you going to have to slow your speed down, we're driving on mixed road," Adrian said.

"And stay in the vehicles at all times until we reach the abandoned base. There still could be traces of mercury from the town's mines," Russell said. The town has a large history of mercury mining, causing environmental concern about its spread of the toxin. "Close all of the vents, and turn on the vehicle's oxygen system. It will help you breathe until we reach the base," Adrian said.

Darrell presses a button near the center console with two curved lines to close the ventilation. He presses a button below it that shows the symbol, O_2 and activates the system. Two small openings go out of the vehicle's body, temporarily exposing them to the outside world as they feel the wind. The openings then close back in, but with a net-like application hooked onto it. The screen on top of the center console turns on, showing the system's oxygen levels at full power. The system converts hazardous airborne materials from the outside as it sucks air into the vehicle. The system also cleans out the inside from impurities that enter it. The system still operates at 100% due to its large and efficient capacity.

As the group is going at cruising speed, they notice the large abandoned base in the distance. The base was moss green as it appeared to stretch to about a half of a mile wide. "How are you guys doing on oxygen?" Russell said.

"Still operating at 100%," Phoenix said.

As they drive closer to the base, they notice a large, white five-digit number imprinted on its left side. "00367?" Darrell said quietly. "Hey, what's the number mean?"

"That means this is the 367th base established in the organization's history," Russell said.

"Is this one of the first bases?" Darrell said.

"Oh, no. There's a hell of a lot more from where these

came from. Why do you think there are five digits?"

Phoenix sighs and says sarcastically, "Wonderful."

The group slows their vehicles down as they arrive at the front entrance. The base was vast in height as they looked up at its highest point. It is around five-hundred feet from their estimate. Adrian and Russell get out of their vehicles and walk towards the entrance. Russell lets his hand out and moves it towards Darrell, indicating to stay in the vehicle. Phoenix started to wonder, "Why does he want us to stay in the vehicle?"

"I don't know, probably trying to get in for us," Darrell said. They notice a blue glow from Russell's wrist communicator near the base's security system.

"Well, I'm going to get out to see what they're doing," Phoenix said.

"No, Phoenix, stay in the car."

"You're not my boss, Darrell. I'm going to get answers."
She attempts to get out of the vehicle, but Darrell catches her.

"Hey," he said. "What are you doing?!" He grabs Phoenix by the arm. She was getting agitated, "Stop it, Darrell!" Phoenix tries to break free from his grip, but only struggles in the process. Darrell pushes her against the seat, "You better quit, Phoenix."

"Who the hell do you think you are?!"

"Going out there will make it worse! You need to learn how to sit tight until the right moment comes to act." Darrell lets go of Phoenix and says angrily, "Put your seat belt on before they see you." Phoenix looks at him with frustration. She forcefully pulls down the seat belt and buckles it, folding her arms.

The blue glow dissipated as the entrance slowly opened. Russell and Adrian turn around and walk to their vehicles. Darrell and Phoenix noticed that Adrian looked uncomfortable as he showed an expression of fear. Darrell rolled down the window and said, "What was that blue glow for?"

"Overrode the system," Russell said quickly. Phoenix widened her eyes in disbelief, picturing a series of possible scenarios in the future. Darrell rolled the window back up. "That crazy bastard," Phoenix said. Darrell shakes his head and sighs.

The massive front entrance doors slowly open to reveal the inside. The group drives through to see the environment around them. There is a large network of newly paved four-lane roads arranged in different sections. The sections appeared to be in the setup of an obstacle course. In front of their sight was a small, black building that appeared to be about fifty feet in height, filling the center of the network of roads. Adrian said through the communication system, "Alright, now what you see here is Stage One of the training session. You will go through a series of challenges that may help you in your next mission. This will test your maneuvering skills and split-second decisions. This course will stretch for miles." Darrell and Phoenix looked at each other in disgust. "The training course will get progressively tougher as you move through it. Russell and I will guide you along the way. This requires concentration in order to pull this off successfully."

Darrell slowly turns to enter the base's roads. He notices a thirty mile per hour speed limit sign as they drive closer to the starting point of the course. "Never thought that a corrupt organization had the courtesy to follow driving laws," Darrell said sarcastically.

"I'm going to ask you guys to stop there. We will set up the base's surveillance system to keep track of your progress. Sit tight, for now, this may take a little while. I'd turn off the gas if I were you," Russell said. Darrell shuts off the vehicle, causing the oxygen system to power down as they were able to breathe normal air.

"Since when did you suddenly care about the environment?" Phoenix said to Russell. No response. Russell and Adrian drive in reverse until they sharply turn to the right. Their rear bumpers face the entrance. They continue in reverse until they face the entrance inside the base. They set their vehicles in drive and go straight to the black building. As they slow down towards the doors of the building, they start to open automatically. They slowly roll in as the doors close behind them.

"So, I'm assuming there are three stages," Phoenix said.

"Driving, Off-road, and Weapons and Tactics," Russell said.

About five minutes have passed by. "What's taking them so long?" Phoenix said.

"Probably setting up," Darrell said.

"Okay, you guys ready?" Adrian said through the communication system.

"Took you long enough," Phoenix said. Russell said, "Don't start yet, all we have to do is set up the obstacles, objectives, and targets. This will only take a moment." Darrell and Phoenix noticed a sign ahead of him with two orange arrows pointing down.

Stage One is now in operation and ready for testing.

"Okay, on my mark after one, that means go," Adrian said.

Darrell starts the vehicle and deactivates the oxygen system.

He activates the launch control and sets it in neutral. "3,"

Adrian said. Darrell slightly revs the vehicle. "2.....1." He

pushes his foot down on the throttle, but not fully. "GO!"

Darrell floors it and feels the sudden jolt from the

acceleration, causing the tires to screech and create smoke.

"After you pass the gate ahead of you, you're going to turn

right," Adrian said.

"And after that, what? Shoot these fuckers?" Phoenix

said.

"Oh, you'll see what we have in store for you," Russell

said.

After Darrell passes the gate, he drifts to the right and

immediately sees two trucks, an orange one, and a black one.

The trucks come out from an underground garage behind

them. Nobody is in the vehicles. "Drone vehicles," Darrell

said. "Take them down, do what you guys do best," Russell said. Darrell activates the rear machine guns with his preferred settings from the pursuit in New York City and fire at the trucks. The trucks immediately took damage after firing, piercing through the trucks' engines. Darrell and Phoenix look at each other and nod. "Just like the good old times," Phoenix said, smiling. "Shoot their tires." Darrell locks onto the tires on the screen and fires. The tires popped only after a couple rounds, but Darrell continued firing. The trucks flew a couple feet in the air and exploded on impact. "Damn, you guys are touchy," Russell said.

"We're just getting started," Phoenix said boldly. They notice a robotic arm quickly come out of the building towards the wrecked trucks. The arm scooped them towards the building and into a large opening, falling into a dark hole.

Darrell drifts to the right. "A tunnel will rise, go in it once it submerges," Adrian said. Darrell keeps driving straight. They notice four vehicles come out, two trucks and two sedans, windows covered. Darrell panics, "Where the fuck is the tunnel?!" The tunnel pops up just in time. "Go in there, now!" Adrian said. As they approach the tunnel, they notice a gate that's similar to the gate in the beginning of the first stage. There are beige tinted lights from the tunnel's ceiling as they entered. The engine's sound echoed as they drove it. "Now, the next section will test your melee skills. No vehicular firearms will be used during this section. However, you can use the vehicle's defense mechanisms to your advantage," Russell said.

"But wouldn't that be the weapons' job?" Darrell said.

"No, like I said before, elite class agents have privileges to everything in the organization. The defense mechanisms will be located at the bottom of the center console."

Darrell drives up a slightly submerged ramp, ending the tunnel. He turns to the right to see the vehicles ahead of him. He draws in close to get between the vehicles with two on each side. He attempts to ram the sedan to his left, but the vehicle barely budges. He presses a button with a horseshoe magnet. The screen above the center console started showing the letters, N or S, indicating the poles. If the magnetism matches or opposes the letter, the driver will be able to push away or attract the pursuers. The magnetism of the pursuers is S. Darrell briefly holds the button in to switch from north to south, emitting a red glow. He lets go and quickly presses the button to release a magnetic pulse, immediately pushing away the vehicles to about seven feet apart. He's now able to ram the sedans. He makes an abrupt turn in both directions to impact the vehicles. This caused one of the sedans to spin out of the control and the other to hit the wall, totaling the drone sedans.

Darrell accelerates until he's in between the trucks. "You may have to increase the power level for the trucks," Russell said. Darrell looks at the screen to notice the word, POWER on the top left side. He taps it to notice a vertical line with a percentage. The power levels are currently operating at 10%. Darrell slowly moves his finger up to a slightly higher percentage. "Let's try 17%," Darrell said. He holds the horseshoe button until it's showing a blue glow, switching to north. He presses the button as the magnetism was strong enough to repel them to about thirty feet, creating a small shock wave. The truck from Darrell's left had significant damage as it impacted a wall. The truck from his right came off course as it was performing a series of barrel rolls. The Lamborghini has minor scratches from the ordeal. "Damn," Darrell said in awe. "I wonder what it's like at 100%."

"I wouldn't try it," Phoenix said as she looked at him firmly.

"Stop the vehicle," Adrian said. Darrell slammed on the brakes until coming to a complete stop. Russell said, "Alright, next is Stage Two. It's not located on Stage One. It will be on the outside. After you get out of that stretch, turn right and wait for the security doors to open. We will open them for you by the time you get there." Darrell drives in the remainder of the stretch as he turns right to steadily decelerate the vehicle. He does this until he's by the security doors away from the opposite side of the entrance.

The security doors slowly open. Darrell slowly turns left to see the environment around him. The environment is completely different than what Stage One offered. He drove into the second course to explore it. He and Phoenix were traveling on a mixed road of dirt and gravel. They are surrounded by several trees of varying heights and other green plants. Russell said, "Since you're going into the wilderness on your next mission, this will give you a head start. The wilderness is like a maze, yet dangerous if not careful. Your enemy could lurk anywhere in the woods and could attack at any moment." Darrell hangs a small right while listening to Russell. "Always keep an eye on your surroundings in any setting involving nature."

Darrell and Phoenix look behind them to notice two armored drone sports utility vehicles pulling in from behind in the distance. They were the Porsches they faced a year ago.

"These bastards again," Phoenix said. They felt a gunshot, but it wasn't from the sports utility vehicles. Phoenix looked in her side mirror to see two armored trucks on a ledge shooting at them. She panicked and rolled her window down. She took her assault rifle off of her back and started firing three round bursts. "Shit!" Darrell panicked.

"You have to pay attention to your surroundings, like I said," Russell said. Phoenix stopped firing. The trucks turn in front of the sports utility vehicles. "Darrell, focus on the trucks first. They're weaker than the SUVs," Phoenix said.

Darrell fires at the trucks with the machine guns, instantly damaging them. As he shot the vehicles' tires, the vehicles flew about five feet in the air, but the SUVs plowed them out of the way like they were nothing. He fired at one of them, but it takes more bullets than the other drones. Right after he weakened one of them, Darrell notices two other vehicles turning in front of the SUVs while traveling at about fifty miles per hour. The vehicles ahead of the SUVs were drawing closer at a quick rate. Darrell and Phoenix panicked.

Phoenix notices a road that hangs to the right. "TURN RIGHT!" She yells. Darrell quickly turns, but the drones keep going in the same direction. Phoenix looks behind her to see the vehicles suddenly colliding with intense force, creating a chain reaction of explosions on impact. Darrell takes a deep breath and sighs while looking in the rearview mirror, "Holy shit."

"And that's what's supposed to happen in the wilderness? Pay attention, my ass," Phoenix said.

Darrell drives into a large open space, noticing several objects in his sight. Him and Phoenix noticed a square, silver metallic platform in the center of the space accompanied by four steel pillars. Darrell stops the vehicle on the platform and waited. "This signifies the end of Stage Two, you may exit out of the forest section," Russell said.

"But, how the hell are we supposed to get out of here? It's blocked by your fucking drones!" Phoenix said.

"Phoenix," Darrell said. He pointed to the other side.

"There's another way out." Phoenix sighs in frustration,

"Goddamnit." Darrell slowly turns and drives to where he

pointed at.

After a series of small turns through the forest section,

Darrell and Phoenix spot the exit. They drive through it to see

the driving course again. "So, where do you want us to go?"

Phoenix said.

"Go into the building," Russell said. Darrell turns to the

left and goes on a straight stretch until he reaches the other

end. He turns again and continues driving until he stops near

the building Russell and Adrian went into. The doors slowly

opened as Darrell drew closer to the building.

Darrell drove into what appears to be pitch black all

around them. Four small lights with one from each direction

immediately turn on. Him and Phoenix looked around to

study their surroundings. The lights revealed dark blue

metallic walls as the ceiling was about thirty feet above them

and another set of doors. "Just sit tight," Russell said. They hear sounds of the clanging of metal and feel the room descend like an elevator.

After the descent, the elevator stops moving. The set doors opened to reveal a dark corridor made of steel being lit from its side. Russell said, "You're now entering the Final Stage of your training. This stage moves away from vehicular combat. This tests your skills in tight situations while on foot. This will also test your acrobatic skills and marksmanship."

Darrell and Phoenix walk out of the elevator to enter the corridor towards the light. The light was coming from the windows by the side, revealing a room with several obstacles. Phoenix cocks her pistol and readies it. "This should be interesting," Phoenix said.

"Just like old times, I'm the fighter, you're the gunner," Darrell said. He looks at Phoenix. "You know, I may have to shoot, too sometime."

"Then let's practice on our team work. I barely saw you shoot a firearm, so we may have to get you one." They walk to a security door. As it opens, there are two drones that share the same appearance as the agents of their organic counterparts. Darrell and Phoenix were startled as the agents were holding two pistols. "That's means now, Darrell," Phoenix said.

"Spoken too soon." They charge at the drones and start attacking. Phoenix shoots a bullet through one of the drone's heads, disabling it instantly. Darrell charges a punch at the other drone, but is interrupted as it grabs his fist. The drone slightly bends his fist backward, but doesn't stun him. Darrell breaks free and charges at the drone by attempting to punch it again. The drone uses its arms to block its upper region. Darrell was getting frustrated. The drone exits its defense position and attempts to throw a right hook. He ducks just in time. The drone pushes him against the wall. "Damn, even drones are a pain in the ass!" Darrell said. Him and Phoenix walk to the door and enter another hallway.

Phoenix noticed three more drones running towards

their way, creating shadows from the bright light reflecting behind them. "What the hell are you waiting for? Shoot it!" Darrell said. The drone looks to its right to notice the others, then focuses back on Darrell. Phoenix pulls the trigger and takes out the drone. She runs to catch up to Darrell as he's running. "You take the one on the left, I'll take the other!" Phoenix said.

Darrell and Phoenix are running side by side as they approach the drones. One of the drones shoot their pistols at Phoenix, which made her tense up. The bullet wasn't penetrable. She was shocked, "What the fuck?" As they meet face to face with the drones, Darrell immediately tackles one of them and drives his fists into its face.

Phoenix runs up the wall and keeps an eye on her drone, which caught Darrell's attention as he performed one last punch on a drone. She grunts as she vaults off of the wall, swiftly kicking the drone in the face. She lets her arm out as she's up in the air to shoot the back of the drone's head. The drone made a loud thud right after Phoenix returned to the ground. Darrell was in shock, "When did you learn to do that?!"

"No time to explain, we have a course to finish. Let's go," Phoenix said. Darrell gets up as Phoenix is already running towards the light. "Hey, wait for me!" Darrell yelled. Phoenix ignored him. Darrell sprints towards her as she charges at the glass doors projecting the light.

Phoenix successfully barges the doors to reveal the room, but doesn't break them. They notice a small corridor as they walk in. She turns around and ducks just in time as she notices a drone's arm coming from the side. Phoenix punches the drone, stunning it and pulls out her assault rifle. She fires a three round burst in the chest. The drone is still operating, but just barely. They also mimic the same characteristics and emotions as a regular human. She shoots one round with her pistol, knocking it to the ground.

Darrell and Phoenix run out of the corridor and enter the

spacious portion of the obstacle course. They notice two more drones running towards them. They quickly stride away from the drones' direction. The drones turn around and run towards them, projecting expressions of anger. Darrell delivers a punch that's hard enough to knock one down to the ground. He notices a few more drones with pistols coming from where they entered by the small corridor. "Phoenix, behind you!" Darrell said. She shoots the drone with her pistol and focuses on the others.

Darrell and Phoenix run towards the drones. Phoenix shoots two of the five in the head. Darrell gets cornered by the remaining three. Phoenix looks around to study the environment around her. There are suspended platforms that were about twenty feet in the air, which is about one-third from the ceiling. There were also walls and thick pillars with no stairs. They were excluded for a reason, to test acrobatics.

Phoenix heard a voice from the room's loudspeaker. "See if you can break him free." It matched Russell's voice. She looks up just below the ceiling to see a brightly lit window to see Russell and Adrian standing there, watching them.

Phoenix gasped. Russell was smiling, but Adrian wasn't, he looked like he was worried about something. She started running to one of the pillars. Darrell was being pulled and pushed from the drones as they were about to pin him down to the ground. Darrell was panicking, "Phoenix, where the hell are you going?!"

"I'm going to try to break you free!" Phoenix yelled.

"Why not just shoot them?!"

"And risk accidentally shooting you instead?!" She runs up the wall and vaults over to a platform that's separated to about three feet off to the side of another platform. The platforms were steep as they give about five feet of width to move on. As she landed on the platform, she stopped running for a brief moment as she noticed Russell still giving a cunning smile. She said to herself angrily, "What are you smiling at, dude?"

Phoenix continues to run while she clings her feet to the wall. She vaults over to a platform as her wall run ended. She's now about fifteen feet above the floor. She notices two more drones with guns coming in from the small corridor. "Oh, great," Phoenix said in disgust. They aim and shoot at Phoenix as she sprints towards the platform ahead of her. They barely miss her. She's sweating from the pressure and grunts as she jumps over a five-foot gap. She lands on the platform and catches her breath.

Phoenix runs to the final platform. As she jumps to the other side, she yells and turns around while in the air, aiming her pistol at the drones by Darrell. The two armed drones shoot at her, causing her to grunt, but didn't penetrate her. She fires two rounds at the drones, one for each, and takes them down without harming Darrell. She turns around again and does a combat roll as she lands on the final platform. The platform was hexagonal in shape, giving her ample room to move around. She walks down the end of the platform and steadily aims at the final drone. Darrell was still struggling as he tried to break free from it while laying on the ground. Phoenix closes one of her eyes and says, "Come on, you bastard, hold still." She fires the round just before the drone tried to turn Darrell around. It let go of Darrell as it thudded to the ground. Phoenix lowered her gun and started breathing heavily.

The other two drones start running towards Darrell as he's slowly rolling over. He said, "Oh fu-" Phoenix shoots the drones, surprising Darrell. Phoenix angrily looks at the window of where Russell is standing, "Fucking BBs? What are you, fifteen?!" Russell points his finger up, "Keyword, training."

"Great, now tell me how I'm supposed to get down? You wouldn't mind telling me that?"

The platform started to lower, causing Phoenix to trip and almost fall. As the platform lowered, Darrell quickly got up on his feet. She ran to Darrell. He yelled, "Are you fucking crazy?!"

"Look, I saved your ass, you should be grateful," Phoenix said, putting her pistol in her pocket.

"This marks the end of your training, let's get out of here," Russell said in a hurry.

"Wait, why so quickly?" Phoenix said.

"We have a mission to do! Let's get out of here!"

Darrell and Phoenix sprint to the corridor and run through the hallways they came from. "We'll meet you outside. Get out of there as soon as you can," Russell said through the communicator.

"What's the rush for?" Darrell said.

"Just trust me."

"I don't know, Darrell. He was smiling earlier for something," Phoenix said. Darrell and Phoenix reach the doors from where they parked their vehicle. The doors opened as they ran towards the Lamborghini. They got in the vehicle while the doors were closing. The elevator begins to ascend. "What the hell's going on?" Darrell said.

"We'll find out soon enough," Phoenix said.

The elevator opens. Darrell sets the vehicle in reverse and backs out at full throttle. He jerks the steering wheel until he faces the entrance doors of the base. "Actually, wait for us, we need to get our vehicles, this will only take a minute," Russell said. Phoenix was growing impatient, "What the hell's the hold-up, Russell?! First, you want us to get out of here, then you want us to fucking wait for you. Make up your GODDAMN mind!"

Suddenly, a loud alarm is sounded throughout the base, followed by a red light from the building. Phoenix gasped and said, "Come on, Darrell. Let's get the fuck out of here!"

Russell and Adrian are just coming out of the building as they are reversing in opposite directions from each other. They are now driving towards Darrell. The group floored it as they exit the base. They are going slightly over one hundred miles per hour to protect the vehicles' wheelbases. They turn left and make another left, entering the asphalt.

As they are turning, they notice a fleet of high-performance vehicles from the distance. "HAHAHA! Motherfuckers didn't see it coming! Got here before they fucking did!" Russell said as him and the rest of the group accelerate on the road. "I thought the base was abandoned," Darrell said.

"Well, apparently not since there's a fleet after us!" Phoenix yelled. Darrell and Phoenix notice the fleet turning to the road leading to the base. "They not coming after us. They probably think we're part of them," Darrell said.

"Don't be fooled, they're probably waiting for us to strike again. It could be anywhere. We have more on our hands now."

"Goddamnit! That son of a bitch!"

"I'm not coming with you guys on this one," Adrian said.

"Why not, Adrian?" Russell said.

"I have shit to get done. Besides, I wasn't part of the job anyways." Adrian accelerates and drives ahead of Darrell and

Russell in the distance.

Phoenix takes a deep breath, "Adrian's right, Russell is fucking crazy. It takes a lot of damn nerve to pull off something like that and get excited about it!" Phoenix takes another deep breath and says, "I'd keep your eyes peeled for Yellowstone, Darrell. There are some things we may have to watch while we're down there." She tenses up, "Ooh! That pisses me off!"

As the group leaves New Idria, they will leave with what they learned for their next mission as they hunt for the target, Conway Barkevich.

Chapter 10: The Wilderness

August 6, 2020

Yellowstone National Park, Montana

Darrell and Russell drive on asphalt while surrounded by trees, stretching for miles. There were no other signs of vegetation, mostly desert and barren terrain. They stopped and turned to enter an ascending hilly road. They were now driving on a dry dirt road. Russell is wearing his business attire along with his sunglasses as Darrell and Phoenix are wearing their black outfits he gave them. "Alright, keep going up this way, this will lead to Sheep Mountain. That's where their base is located," Russell said. "There's something that I want you guys to do by the time we get up there."

"And what would that be?" Phoenix said arrogantly.

"It won't be easy to get in. I'm going to pretend to turn you in to the organization." Phoenix got tense and got angry, "What the hell are you doing, Russell? First, you lie about an abandoned base. Now, you want us to risk our lives against possibly hundreds of agents?"

"Phoenix, they'll think we captured you. I'll be taking you in the holding room, but there's a weapon storage room right next to it. If we can get in without compromising our cover, then we'll be able to take Conway down and get a few more weapons."

"Hah, just in time for Darrell to get some target practice." Darrell looks at Phoenix, confused.

Darrell and Russell stop ascending as they enter another dirt road circling around on the top of the mountain. They didn't see as many trees when they turned. There was mostly dirt and rock as it was out in the open. They reduce to cruising speed to avoid suspicion. They stop and turn to enter the asphalt. They notice a base from their right as it appeared

to be a hundred feet tall. "Speed up a little bit, make it look

like you're being chased," Russell said.

Darrell accelerated as he switched to second gear. Russell

accelerated, but kept a distance from the Lamborghini. They

were fast approaching the base, which is dark green. "Stop

and turn right!" Russell yelled suddenly. His voice startled

Darrell and Phoenix, causing them to jump and yell. Darrell

slammed the brake and turned, leaving a trail of smoke. They

stopped in front of the base's large security doors.

Russell caught up to Darrell and parked his vehicle next

to the Lamborghini. They look up and spot the base's

establishment number, 00519. Russell quickly gets out of his

Nissan and runs to Darrell. Russell opens the door and

snatches Darrell, "Put these on!" He has two pairs of

handcuffs. He quickly fastens the cuffs around his wrists, but

doesn't lock them. Russell now focuses on Phoenix. She

panics and opens the door. "Yeah, that's it, you better run, because I'm coming for you!"

"Help! Help!" Phoenix yelled as she was running. Russell sprinted towards Phoenix as he moves around the Lamborghini. He charges and grabs her. Phoenix struggles while in Russell's hold and says, "What are you doing?!"

"Shut up! You're by the building now!" Russell yelled.

"Fuck you, Russell!"

"Put the cuffs on!"

"I ain't your fucking proper-" Phoenix was interrupted. Russell snapped and whispered in Phoenix's hair, "I said, put! Them! ON!"

"Just do what he says, Phoenix!" Darrell yells. Phoenix breathes heavily and calms down. She puts her arms behind her. Russell takes the handcuffs and fastens them around her wrists. Like with Darrell, he doesn't lock them. Russell grabs Phoenix and walks to Darrell, "Come on, this will only take a moment."

Russell walks up to the touchpad towards the side of the

doors. He types in the twenty digit code and waits for the confirmation. The screen said ACCESS GRANTED, causing the doors to slowly open. "Don't do anything stupid," Russell said quietly. He walks Darrell and Phoenix into the base.

Russell saw a large group of formally dressed agents along with a roster of military vehicles surrounding them. There were traditionally green armored vehicles and tanks neatly arranged, covering all four sides of the base's interior. Russell stopped walking as Darrell and Phoenix stopped with him. The agents started walking and lined up from both sides as they made a straight path to a small tan building. The three looked around to see all of the agents. One of the agents stepped out of line and slowly walked to Russell, "Mr. Barkevich." The agent salutes to eye level. Darrell and Phoenix look angrily at the agent. "Job well done." Russell salutes back. Phoenix looks at Russell in disgust. The agents stride to move out of the way. The agent said, "Direct them to the holding room."

Russell takes Darrell and Phoenix to the holding room

ahead of them as the agent walks beside them. As they stop

towards the holding room's entrance, the agent walks ahead

of them. "I'll open the doors for you." He walks to the

touchpad and enters a ten digit code. "*Tst*, how nice of you,

you piece of shit," Phoenix said to the agent. The agent

ignores her.

The agent pushes the doors open to reveal a room that's

similar to a sheriff's office. The walls were white as the floor

was also white. There are a few chairs beside the doors as

there was a black haired, white skin-colored agent working

behind a wood-stained desk about five feet ahead of them.

Darrell, Russell, Phoenix, and the agent sit down on the

chairs. The room is about fifty feet wide. A couple more

agents were walking from the opposite side of the desk. "Get

up," Russell said quietly to Darrell and Phoenix. He directs

them to the desk. The desk agent was sitting in front of a

computer, typing.

Darrell and Phoenix were startled as Russell loudly slams his fist on the desk to get the agent's attention. This caused the agent to jerk and turn around in petrification. He then calmed down, thinking it's Conway. He gets up from his office chair and walks to the counter, "Mr. Barkevich, I see that you got the targets. Johnson, what's the report?" The desk agent was talking to the agent beside Russell. "They just came in as Barkevich followed with the salute," Johnson said.

"Nice place for a bunch of fucking lowlives," Phoenix said.

"You better shut up and sit tight, you little bitch," the desk agent said. Phoenix spits in the desk agent's face, "Kiss my ass." The desk agent felt the saliva, making him angry, "You're not much of a talker today, are you, Barkevich?"

Russell sighs, "You know, it doesn't feel so good to be hacked on, does it?" The agent became petrified again, realizing it's not Conway. Conway has a different voice than Russell. "It's good to be back in the organization." Darrell and

Phoenix quietly uncuff themselves and break free from them, but pretend to still be cuffed to avoid blowing their cover.

"Because when it comes to people like you, I'll enjoy every fucking moment, by kicking your sorry ass."

The agent starts getting nervous and breathes heavily. Russell leaps over the desk. The desk agent takes a couple steps back. Johnson yells, "Conway, what are you doing?!" Darrell and Phoenix quickly take their arms away from their back and go after the agent beside them. Darrell tackles Johnson to the ground and pins him down.

The desk agent pulls out his modified pistol. Russell is deeply angered by this. He charges at the desk agent and violently pushes him to the computer, giving no time to react. Russell violently punches the agent in the ribs and head and throws him to the other side of the counter. He performs a devastating left hook on the agent before knocking him out cold, making him thud to the floor. Russell crouches down and grabs his pistol in his hand.

As Darrell was punching Johnson in the face, Phoenix draws her pistol from the inside of her jacket and shoots a clean hole through Johnson's head. The agents around the room were startled and immediately pull out their weapons and aim them all at Darrell, Phoenix, and Russell. Phoenix wasn't petrified.

They immediately shoot at the agents surrounding them. The room becomes a kill zone as they both shoot the agents in the ribs and head. Executing this action resulted in only a couple agents standing while holding assault rifles. Russell ducks before the agents shoot at him and turn their attention towards Darrell and Phoenix. She quickly shoots at both of the agents in the head as they thud to the ground, dropping their weapons. Russell and Phoenix breathe heavily and look around as there were no other agents in sight. "The weapons are by the door ahead of you!" Russell said. "I'll be behind you guys."

Darrell and Phoenix run to the door in the middle of the

room and budge through it. They see a long brightly lit hallway with an arranged assortment of modified weapons sitting on top of display tables from both sides. The walls were white. The light weapons included pistols, assault rifles, shotguns, and sniper rifles. The heavier weapons included rocket launchers and vehicle mounted weapons. They looked around to see the different types of guns. "Now would be a good time to pick a weapon, Darrell," Phoenix said. He walks around to look at the weapons, particularly the pistols. "Never really held a gun in my life," Darrell said.

"Well, you need to learn how to defend yourself under the line of fire. It's really easy with the pistols, Darrell. Doesn't require much to learn from it." Darrell looks at the large assortment of pistols as they were white, gray, silver, and black, each with a matte finish. Depending on the color, each one has a different modification. "Phoenix, all of them have different colors. The colors must mean something," Darrell said.

"Just pick one, we don't have time to experiment!"

Phoenix yells. She walks to Darrell and checks out the pistols.

She picks up another silver one and places it inside her jacket.

Darrell takes a white pistol. Phoenix is startled as she sees

Russell opening the door while breathing heavily, holding the

desk agent's pistol. He enters the hallway. Phoenix gets

irritated and shakes her head negatively, "You're so fucking

slow." Russell closes the door.

"Come on, let's go! They'll be coming any moment! We'll

need all of the firepower we can get!" Russell said. They

sprint through the hallway until Phoenix goes to the assault

rifles to pick up another one similar to what she already has.

They run to a white door as Russell types in the combination.

The door slowly opens automatically. "Does every door have

a combination?! What could they be protecting?!" Phoenix

yelled.

"That's why we're here, Phoenix," Russell said. They run

down the small steps and enter a large garage. Ahead of them was a garage door that was already opened. The door is a

hundred feet tall and five hundred feet wide. The clear skies

were bright enough to illuminate the contents of the garage.

There were militant vehicles that were neatly arranged as

there were armored infantry vehicles, tractor units, and

tanks. There were also enclosed trailers composed of steel

laid off to one side of the garage. Darrell and Phoenix were

both in shock and awe. "Looks like this is where the tanks

came from," Phoenix said.

The group sprints to the tractor units towards the edge

of the garage. They climbed into the vehicle and saw the

interior. There were two seats that are cushioned as they

were primarily made of steel. There was an assortment of

buttons lit with different colors for the vehicle's controls. The

windshield and windows were made of bulletproof glass. The

interior was primarily made of metal as there was also a roll

cage. The units were in the moderate range as they had the

same features from the fleets in New York City. Moderate

class vehicles only have one weapon along with touchscreens

on the dashboard with targeting systems for the front and rear. By Phoenix on the passenger side is a handlebar with a red button on each end that controls the weapon systems. There were buttons around the handle bar that are used to switch weapons and types of ammunition.

Darrell gets frustrated and says, "Now, how the hell do you start this thing?" He looks around the steering wheel to find a small lever. "Hmm, well that's new." IFHR removed the key ignition for the trailer units and exchanged it with a lever mechanism for quicker start-ups. He pulls down the lever, unsure if the vehicle will start. He holds it down for a few seconds and hears the roar of an engine. "We're going to attach the trailers," Russell said through the communicator. Darrell and Russell back up until they are in front of the trailers.

While the group got out to attach the trailers, agents storm the garage's entrance. The group was shocked. "Get them!" one of the agents yelled. The agents run after them.

They fire at the agents as they focus on the trailer hitches. Phoenix dual-wields her pistols as she fires them simultaneously in an alternating pattern. Darrell slowly pulls out his weapon. "Just point and shoot," Phoenix said. He raises his weapon and aims at the agents. The bullets from Darrell's pistol were scorching hot as they were orange.

The bullets then scattered into smaller segments, killing three agents, one in the neck, and the others in the skull. Blood was gushing out from an agent's neck as it splattered to the floor. The three agents thudded to the ground. Half of the agents are already killed as Russell just draws his weapon. Phoenix was shocked as her jaw dropped and saw the damage. Russell didn't seem surprised from the damage of Darrell's pistol. Phoenix gave Russell an angry look as he was shooting the remaining agents. He wasn't paying attention to her. The group stops firing and put the tow balls inside the trailers' hitches. "Come on, let's go!" Russell yelled.

The group hops into their vehicles and drive to the end

of the garage, leaving small amounts of smoke from the roofs' exhaust tips. The tractor units have a lifted chassis for improved suspension with thirty-six-inch tires and off-road capabilities. The aggressive haul of the tractors' engines emanated throughout the garage's interior. They turn and head for the entrance of the base. Phoenix noticed the word, CONNECTED briefly appear on the screen. "Connected?" she said. "What does that mean?" Darrell notices agents from both sides of the vehicles holding an assortment of firearms. "No time to guess right now, we have more important things to worry about!" Russell said.

Phoenix activates the machine guns and fire at the agents in the distance. Russell and Darrell briefly turn to the lines of agents and run a couple of them over. The tractor units violently rammed them with their silver chrome grilles, breaking their bones and fracturing their skulls as the tires' hard rubber crush their bodies.

They stopped at the base's entrance to see that their

vehicles were still intact. They notice another tractor unit with a trailer approaching the entrance. A sky blue Maserati sedan was driving behind it. The unit and the sedan stopped in the middle of the road as the back of the trailer lowered its door. The Maserati was driving on the inclined plane of the trailer to enter it.

A bald man wearing sunglasses runs down the inclined plane. "Who the hell is that?" Darrell said. The man looks behind him and spots the group. He panics and sprints towards the driver's side of the unit while the plane is rising up. Russell sees him opening the door and pushing the driver aside while unbuckling his seat belt. Something snaps in Phoenix's mind. She gasps, "Wait a second, that's Conway!"

"Don't let him get away!" Russell said through the communicator. Conway drives off of the asphalt and onto the dirt road beside the base to enter the woods. The Maserati has off-road tires and suspension. The group straightens their tractor units as they stop them in the middle of the road. The units were at the entrance as they were close to the group's vehicles. Darrell and Russell pulled a lever just above the throttle to open the door of the trailers as the doors whistled. The group got out and ran to their vehicles.

The group sees agents run up towards the tractor units with firearms. Darrell and Phoenix tensed up as they fired at the agents, already killing a couple of them. A couple agents fire their assault rifles at them. Darrell and Phoenix sprint to the bottom of the trailer and get into cover. They crawl into the bottom as they hide in between the axle of the front of the trailer. They shoot the agents in the legs as they immediately fall to the ground.

Phoenix notices Russell still standing in the line of fire as he's giving an expression of anger. He runs around the entrance as he quickly shoots the agents in the heads and chests. "Come on, you motherfuckers!" Russell yells. He breathes heavily as he looks at the dead agents.

Russell notices that one of the agents are still alive. The

agent is coughing up blood as there was a bullet hole cut clean through his chest. He slowly walks to the agent as his anger was growing, flowing through his entire body. "Russell, what the hell are you doing?!" Darrell said. Russell's state of animosity blurred him as he ignored Darrell and crouched down to the agent. "Russell, we have to go!" Darrell attempts to get out from under the trailer, but Phoenix grabbed a hold of him. She pulls him back under the trailer and pushes him down. She whispers, "DON'T move a fucking muscle!"

Russell looks down at the agent as the agent's eyes reddened from the bullet wound. Russell shot him directly in the heart as his chest was slowly bleeding out. He vigorously grabs the agent by the collar of his suit jacket and lifts him from the ground. Russell was still breathing heavily as he grinned his teeth. He brought the fear in the agent's eyes as the agent was shaking from the blood loss. The agent's face reddened as he gagged from the blood in his mouth. The agent slowly closed his eyes and made a shallow breath as he died. Russell lets go of him as the agent made a small thud on the asphalt of the entrance. Blood started to spread from the agent's body as Russell looked down on him one last time.

Russell looked up as he woke from his vexation, sprinting to his unit. He looked back and noticed Darrell and Phoenix under their unit and yelled, "What the hell are you guys doing?! We have a target to kill!" The group ran to their vehicles they originally came in and backed them up into the trailers. The interior of the trailers was silver as there were steel mechanical bars forming an X and a plus sign crossed together on the ceiling. Darrell and Russell hear a whistling sound from the ceiling. Phoenix looks up to see what it is. "Oh, shit!" she panics. "That thing's gonna fucking crush us. Let's get out of here, now!" They bolt out of the Lamborghini. Phoenix executes a combat roll as they saw that the mechanical bars were halfway above the trailer's floor and sprinted down the inclined plane. Russell was already out of the trailer as he looked at its interior. Darrell and Phoenix look in the trailer to see the mechanical bars touching their vehicle's roof. The metal of the bars was flexible and durable.

They weren't damaging the vehicle as they followed and molded to the shape of it. The bars protect the vehicle from being damaged during transportation and emergency situations.

The group saw agents running towards the base from a far distance. Russell also noticed a couple tractor units with the IFHR insignia and infantry vehicles along with a couple armored pickup trucks driving towards the base. The infantry vehicles and trucks have raised suspension kits and large tires for enhanced off-road capabilities. The group ran to their tractor units and drive towards the fleet of vehicles blocking their way. They shoot at the trucks with the units' machine guns. The trucks shoot back as Darrell and Russell T-bones them out of the way, totaling them as they enter the woods. The rest of the opposing vehicles turn around to follow the group.

The woods are filled with winding pathways and trees as sunlight delivered spots onto the ground. Phoenix looks back to notice the vehicles behind her, "Shit, they're behind us!"

Darrell and Russell activate the rear machine guns and shoot

at their pursuers. The pursuing vehicles return the favor by

shooting at them.

The group and the pursuing vehicles enter a straightaway

on the dirt road. In the distance, there is a couple armored

pickup trucks side by side on small hills above them. They

accelerate down the hills as the group heard the trucks'

boisterous engines and drive beside their tractor units. Darrell

and Phoenix look at each other. "Just like old times," Phoenix

said. They nodded their heads. Darrell looks down at the

truck beside him and rolls his window down. He aims and

shoots at the window and tires. The bullets shattered the

glass, penetrating it after a couple shots. Darrell rams the

truck by the side, throwing it off course. The truck loses

traction and hits a tree in the distance head-on, rendering it

useless. Russell rams the truck beside him as the truck skids,

but recovers quickly.

The group returns to the pattern of winding turns. As Russell makes a hard turn, his trailer approaches the truck, knocking it sideways and making it do a couple barrel rolls. "And they say no big trucks allowed," Darrell said.

The group focuses their attention on the infantry vehicles and tractor units behind them. They lock on the tractor units and resume firing. The bullets do their damage, but it wasn't significant. The bullets were only able to make engravings and chip off parts of their grilles, but the engines weren't affected. The group stops firing for a brief moment. Darrell and Phoenix were getting frustrated. "Damn it, they're not fucking budging!" Darrell said.

The group resumes firing as they only chip off more small pieces of the grilles. They stop firing again. "Son of a fucking bitch!" Phoenix said. Darrell hits the steering wheel in frustration, "It's no use."

"Speed up," Russell said.

"How are we supposed to speed up if we're going

through a FUCKING maze?!" Phoenix yelled.

"There will be a straightaway when we exit this turn." Phoenix suddenly became curious, "Wait a second, how do you know where to go every single time?" Russell was getting angry, "Just listen to me before they blow our goddamn asses up!"

The group turns left and go on the straightaway. They look in the rear-view mirrors to notice the fleet right behind them. "Now drive!" Russell said.

"Hang on," Darrell said to Phoenix as he grips his hand on the chrome silver gear stick in between the center console. Darrell and Russell slammed the throttle as the engines echoed throughout the woods. The group just switch into the high gears as the supercharged engines climb up to almost a hundred miles per hour. The agents start to lose their distance with the group. The agents fired as the group continued to evade them. The group continues to accelerate as they were a couple hundred feet away.

The group sees an arch with curved trees that reveal the bright sun and grass as it was a few feet shorter than the roofs of the tractor units. The group plows through the arch as they slightly damage it by expanding the opening. The arch revealed a large and circular area surrounded by trees, bushes, and grass. "Let's go in the section beside us and hide in the shadows. We're going to cut them," Russell said. As they hang a left, their pursuers just emerge from the damaged arch, but they already spotted them.

The group enters through another arch, leading to a new section of forest. The agents thrust their brakes and stop in the middle of the circular area. The group slightly turn away from each other as they stop beside trees. "Ready your knives, we're going to ambush them," Russell said as they got out of the vehicles.

The group jumps down from the vehicles. "Better find a hiding place quick. Once you know your instincts, you just might survive in the wilderness," Russell said brazenly.

Phoenix notices him still giving the expression from when he looked down on the dying agent, "Tell me something I don't know." The group runs to the closest bushes just beside the arch, away from each other. Russell was alone as Darrell and Phoenix were together. They crouch down and hide in the middle of the bushes as they take out their knives from inside their jackets.

Four agents get out of their vehicles and sprint towards the arch. "It takes balls to get into a place like this," one of the agents yell out. "You can't hide forever." The agents enter through the arch and stop running. The agents look around as they see the group's tractor units parked in the distance. The head of the agent squad was Brant Abrams. He had a medium build like the rest of his squad. He also has buzzed, red hair. All agents were beside each other. "Agents, search the units. I'll look for the targets," Abrams said.

The agents run up to the tractor units as Abrams looks on. He connects his hands behind his back and turns around.

"So, Arkwright! It's been a *LONG* time since you were first on

the run," Abrams said. He starts walking towards the bushes.

"How do you like it? It's gotta feel good if you're gutsy enough

to help a supposed target." He paces around as he's standing

about thirty feet between the bushes. "I've always known you

loved to kill. *Damn* psycho you are." Abrams shrugs, "But, no

biggie. Nothing wrong with having anger issues in the

organization. It's very common. Very, *very* common."

Abrams walks a couple steps closer to where Russell is

hiding under, moving away from Darrell and Phoenix. Darrell

and Phoenix were hiding in separate bushes beside each

other. They peek to see that Brant has his back turned.

Phoenix firmly looks at Darrell and points her finger between

her lips. She whispers and points at the tractor units, "Going

this way." Abrams resumes, "Remember that time when you

threw a fit and decided to fight one of your fellow agents?"

Phoenix brings her arm to herself, signaling the action to

move. Darrell and Phoenix slowly start moving towards the

tractor units as they're still crouched. "WOO! You fucked him right UP! Almost punched his FUCKING eye out! Eyes were so damn swelled, he couldn't see for THREE months! All because YOU wanted shit YOUR WAY!"

About halfway towards the tractor units, Phoenix notices the agents walking beside the doors. She presses both buttons on the knife to release the main blade and curved blades, creating a loud sheathe. Abrams heard it, which made him turn his back to look at the tractor units, but the agents didn't hear it. "There's nothing here, Abrams," one of the agents shouts. Abrams shifts his eyes to look around the bushes. "Keep looking, they could be anywhere!" Abrams yells.

Phoenix and Darrell see the agents walking towards the front of the vehicles. "Stand up," Phoenix whispers. "Walk slowly." They slowly walk to the sides of the units as the agents had their back turned. "You're fucking pathetic, Arkwright. You think you're all that? You're nothing but a fucking coward," Abrams said. "You know, I've always liked this game of cat and mouse, more fun and thrilling! But it doesn't always have to do with just running around in the backyard in your childhood days."

Darrell and Phoenix sneak up behind the agents as they walk towards the front bumpers. Abrams walks closer to the bush Russell's hiding in, pulling out his pistol. "And I bet you're hiding under there, waiting to chop me up like a crazy ass kitchen butcher. The butcher who constantly bitches about staining his precious little apron." Russell quietly pulls out his knife, preparing it for Abrams. "Chippity-chop, chippity-chop,' Abrams said boldly. Russell quickly jumps out and grabs him with no reaction time.

Phoenix turns around to the front bumper to ready her knife. She quickly stabs the agent in the back of his collar bone, piercing his suit jacket and the deepest layer of skin. The agent screams in pain. She turns the agent around and performs a hard left hook to his cheek, almost knocking him off balance. The agent standing from the other unit panics as he watches.

The agent starts to run to his aid, but he was caught off guard as he heard a loud sheathe behind him. Darrell stabbed the agent in the back, causing the agent to yell and gargle from the puncture. Phoenix charges at the agent she targeted and quickly slashes him two times in the chest as the sun was shining down on her. She knees him in the diaphragm, causing him to bend over. She uppercuts the agent with the knife and stabs a clean cut through his neck, gargling from the damage. She takes the knife out as she swiftly kicked him to the ground.

Darrell turns his agent around and performs a right hook to his face, causing him to fall flat on the ground. Darrell runs up to the agent and pins him down. He charges his fists to his face as he already leaves a black eye. He takes the knife with both hands and raises it upward. He quickly lowers the knife and stabs him in the neck, killing him execution style.

The agent standing in between the tractor units panics

and yells, "Abrams, they're here! Help!"

"Shit, I forgot, there's one more!" Phoenix whispers. She and Darrell run to the middle of the units and spot the agent. The agent turns his back to see Russell holding Abrams hostage. "Hello!" Darrell said boldly, causing the agent to turn around.

"Remember our faces? We're back for more!" Phoenix said. The agent turns around again and panics, "ABRAMS!" The agent sprints away from the tractor units as Darrell and Phoenix follow him, throwing a couple of daggers at him. They just miss him.

The agent stops as he's close to Abrams. Russell was holding his knife at Abrams' neck with a tight grip. Russell aims at the agent with his pistol as Darrell and Phoenix are behind him. The agent shakes and trembles in fear. "Guess, who's back," Russell said. The agent became surprised and petrified as he noticed his voice differed from Conway's. Russell shoots the agent in the forehead, causing him to roll his eyes back and thud to the ground.

Russell becomes enraged as he focuses his attention towards Abrams. Darrell and Phoenix don't even try to intervene. Russell stabs Abrams in the collar bone and grins his teeth, "So, you think this is all a game, huh?!" Abrams grunts from the pain. He stabs him in the ribs, "Apparently you failed to find the mouse's tail!" Russell pulls the knife out and stabs him in the back. "Picking them off one by one! Heh, that's the only thing you guys ever knew!" He pulls the knife out as Abrams gargles from the blood coming out of his mouth. He returns the knife to Abrams' neck, "Remember that time when I escaped from the organization?! Let this be a message to you and every one of your pathetic colleagues at IFHR." He gets close to his ear, but doesn't whisper, "I! WILL! HAVE! MY REVENGE!" He quickly slices Abrams' neck, making him gurgle loudly and widening his eyes. Russell's hand was covered in blood as a couple drops hit his face. The blood rains down Abrams' neck and spills onto his suit jacket. Abrams kneeled and thudded to the ground as his blood spreads. Russell looked down at his dead body as his nose was flaring. Darrell and Phoenix were surprised as their eyes were wide open. "Holy shit!" Darrell whispered.

The group heard loud roars of engines coming from behind them. Two black tractor units and two silver armored pickup trucks emerge from separate arches in the circular area. Russell snaps out of his enraged state and says, "That must be Conway, we gotta go!" They sprint towards the tractor units and get into them.

They set the units in reserve and go full throttle out of the forest section. Once they enter the circular area, they turn in opposing directions and move away from each other, almost hitting the agents' vehicles they confronted. The agents enter the arch from the other side as they disappear from the group's sight. The group straightens their tractor units and face each other. Darrell was backing up as his trailer hit the bushes and almost hit a tree. "This is why I don't want to be a fucking truck driver!" He yells. They turn and head towards the direction of the agents as they shift into low gears. Darrell and Russell keep turning until they are beside each other and break through the arch, capturing the vehicles in the distance.

The armored pickup trucks turned and separated from each other as they drive up small hills beside the trail. The roads were bumpy as Darrell and Russell could hear the tractor units shake. The trucks decelerate until they are beside the group. Darrell aims at the truck's window and fires a couple rounds. The bullets made tiny cracks into the bulletproof window, but barely penetrates. He shoots one round at the tire as the scattershot shreds the rubber. The agent tries to slam on the brake and turn, but was going too fast to react. "Fooled ya!" Darrell yells. The agent went into a skid and crashed into the thick trunk of a tree.

The truck beside Russell shoots a couple rounds at him. The truck begins to accelerate ahead of him, gaining distance from the group and closer to the agents' tractor units. The agents' tractor units were gaining speed, drastically increasing distance from the group as the pickup truck joins them. "Why the hell are they speeding up?" Phoenix said. Suddenly, the units drive downhill and quickly approach a large, hilly ramp as they jump high in the air.

The pickup attempts to drive down to ground level, but reacted too quickly as the agent lost traction and entered into a skid. He goes over the ramp, instantly entering a series of barrel rolls. The group couldn't see the truck as the ramp blocked their vision. "Speed up now," Russell said. The group shifts into the high gears and slam on the throttle.

The barrel rolls stopped as the truck lays on its side, away from the ramp. The vehicle was severely dented as part of the front bumper was coming off. The driver inside was coughing as he had blood stains and bruises on his face. "Shit," The driver said, grunting. "Son of a bitch, that hurt!" He unbuckles the seat belt and almost falls on the passenger beside him. The passenger couldn't move as he was just as damaged as him. "You alright?" the driver asks the passenger. The passenger heard the sound of engines growing louder, "What the hell do you think?" The group emerges from the ramp as they rise from the air. The driver looks up to see the chassis and large wheels of the trailers quickly coming down towards the damaged truck. The driver panics, "OH, SH-" The rear of the trailer impacts the truck and flattens it as it smashes the agents alive.

The group and the remaining agents go through a small and open section of the forest and reenter in the shadows. The group and the agents continue shooting at each other. The group barely leaves any dents in the trailer. Phoenix was getting frustrated. She aims at the wheels and pops a couple tires in one of the trailers. The agent's unit was still going strong, but was slowing down steadily. "Great, now how are we supposed to get him out of the way?" Phoenix said. "Slow down," Russell said.

Darrell slows down as he tries to create a gap for Russell

to turn in. He barely squeezed through as he's driving beside the agent's tractor unit. Darrell speeds up until he is a few feet behind Russell. Russell shoots a couple rounds at the agent's window, but barely penetrates. Not able to reach the tires, he starts ramming the agent repeatedly. The trailers were continuously swerving, concerning Darrell and Phoenix. "What the hell is he doing?" Phoenix said. Russell gives one more invigorating turn and the driver gives in. The agent's unit skids and hits a tree and some bushes as its trailer is slanted off to the side, temporarily blocking Darrell's sight.

Darrell carefully turns away from the agent's trailer and catches up with Russell. The group turns again and speeds up until Russell is beside the other unit. "Stay right there, guys," Russell said.

"Russell, what do you think you're doing?" Phoenix said.

Russell looks to his side and aims his pistol at a bald agent. It was Conway. They go down a hill and drive towards an arch. They enter another circular area surrounded by trees and bushes. In the middle of the area, there was a small gray trapezoidal building. "You're dead, Conway," Russell said boldly.

Russell shoots a couple rounds at Conway's window, warning him. He then shoots the two tires on his side, causing the dirt to build up on the rims. Darrell saw Conway's trailer tip over, causing Phoenix to panic. She gasps and says, "LOOK OUT!" Darrell panics and abruptly turns away from the trailer and enters the arch.

Russell and Darrell stop their vehicles as Darrell parks beside Russell. Conway gets out of his unit and sprints to the building. Russell goes after him. Darrell and Phoenix follow him as they vault over the small barriers surrounding the building.

Russell tackles Conway and pins him down as he starts flying fists at his head. He was enraged as he was instantly creating bruises on his nose and eyes. Conway was trembling in fear. Darrell and Phoenix jump over the barriers again until they are beside Russell. Russell grins his teeth and grabs

Conway's neck. Conway grabs his arm, but Russell performs a

hard left hook, making him go into whiplash. Russell takes out

his knife and stabs him in the diaphragm. Conway grunts as

he puffs his face and feels the pain. "I'm BACK!" Russell said,

stabbing him again. Conway coughs as he gargles from the

blood coming out of his mouth. Blood was coming out of his

diaphragm profusely as Russell looks down on the wound.

"You'll.... never...... get.... away with this.........., Arkwright!"

Conway said. Russell gets close in his face, "I already did." He

stabs him in the heart as Conway loudly gargles. He rattles as

his body was going into shock, killing him, with blood

splattering his face.

Russell breathes heavily and gets up. He was still enraged

as he smeared the blood from his face. Phoenix runs up to

Russell and says, "What the hell is wrong with you?!" Russell

ignores her. Phoenix snaps her fingers, "Hello, are you fucking

there?!"

"We have to get out of here," Russell said, snapping out of his state.

"What were you hiding, Russell? Is there something you're not telling us?" Darrell said.

"Let's just say I caused a lot of trouble in the organization that Adrian and I will never pay back."

"What are you trying to say, Russell?" Phoenix said.

"If you were in the organization, you would know what the hell's up. Now let's get out of here. We'll go in the paths from where we came from. Come on." The group run to their units and turn towards the direction of the arch. They drive into the network of winding paths until they find their way out of the forest.

The group arrives at the base, but there were no agents in sight. They park the units towards the entrance as the base's doors were closed. The trailers were crooked to the side as they were almost touching the roads. They release the back doors of the trailers and get out. The mechanical bars were straightening and rising as their vehicles were free with no damage. They run up the inclined planes and get in the vehicles. They immediately roll out of the trailer and drive away from the base, leaving the trailers opened. "I'm not too sure about this, Darrell," Phoenix said.

"Adrian was right. He is crazy. Maybe there could be a reason behind all of it. Like he said before," Darrell said.

"Maybe, there's always a reason to everything. Things like this don't just happen, but I'm not going to get my hopes up. No matter how many missions we go on, I'm still going to keep my eye on him. I still don't trust that man."

The group exits Sheep Mountain of Yellowstone, eventually returning to California.

Chapter 11: Acquisition

August 8, 2020

Downtown Los Angeles, California

Darrell and Russell pull into the garage as they see Adrian washing tools by the sink. Adrian turns around as they walk up to him, "How'd it go?" He sees blood stains on Russell's face. He stares Adrian down as he enters his enraged state.

"Killed him," Russell whispers loudly. Adrian gave him a disgusted look, "You feeling alright, man?"

"More than I'll ever be." Adrian slams his tools down on the sink, "Alright, you know what, what's your problem? You staring me down is really pissing me off!"

"Russell, stop!" Phoenix yells. Russell doesn't say

anything. "I'm going to get cleaned up and wipe this mess off of my face," Russell said.

"Okay, then. You do that." Russell slowly walks away from the group and enters the kitchen. They all look at him. Darrell and Phoenix walk up to Adrian. "What the hell is his problem?" Adrian said.

"Well, he decided to go crazy on Conway. So, he killed him execution style with his knife. That was real pleasant seeing up close," Phoenix said.

"See? I told you he was crazy." He went back to washing his tools.

"He did say something about you and him, though, while we were out," Darrell said. Adrian stopped the faucet and turned around, "Oh, really? What did he say?"

"He said that you guys did something that you'll never be able to pay back. That most likely needs a lot of explaining to do," Phoenix said. Adrian sighs and briefly looks down.

"Russell recently got into trouble with the organization.

He didn't want to pay attention to what he was told, so he decided to retaliate."

"How'd he get into trouble?"

Russell walks in the garage, startling them, "Come on, guys. There's another mission for you."

Phoenix turns to look at Russell, "We just did one, Russell. It's time to take a break!"

"I don't care, there's something we need to take care of!"

"Give it a rest, Russell! Does it always have to be about you?!" Adrian said. Russell walks up to him, "This doesn't concern you, Adrian. I helped you get out and this is how you talk to me?! I was trying to keep you safe! You're the mechanic and you're supposed to fix things instead of making shit worse than it has to be!"

"And you're *so* bad, you're supposed to be this big shot, aren't you?!"

"Bigger balls than you do!" Adrian shakes his head, "This is why we never get along, Russell. You treat the people around you like pieces of shit." Russell just stares Adrian

down, "Come on, Darrell and Phoenix." They look at Adrian

and sigh. They slowly turn around and follow Russell into the

kitchen and in the computer room.

Russell turns on the computers as he sits down on the

office chair. As they boot up, the database immediately

displays the map. "Your next mission will be hiding out on the

bottom of the East Coast," Russell said.

"I kind of figured since our previous ones jumped from

different places," Phoenix said.

"Yes, they were scattered, but for a reason." Phoenix

raised her eyebrow, nonverbally questioning his statement.

Russell looks at Phoenix, "To conceal their identities. People

have been talking about it for a few years now, but they still

don't know the organization's secrets."

"They'll probably find out about it from when we took

out Arden," Darrell said.

"Maybe, but authorities will most likely think that the

closest relation is a sadistic homicide," Russell said.

Russell looked around the map until he was in the East Coast. The screen pops up with a woman's face on the side. The woman has brown hair and was white in skin color. Russell was staring at the woman's picture as he placed his hand just above his mouth, "Hmm, looks like we found our target already."

"Who is it?" Darrell said.

"It's a woman this time, which could make it an interesting fight for you guys." Russell looks at Phoenix and makes a cunning smile, "Especially for you."

"Is that supposed to be a sexist joke?" Phoenix got angry.

"Now calm down, Phoenix. I haven't mentioned the details yet." Darrell and Phoenix walk up to the computer. "Her name is Rose Takeuchi."

"Is she from around here?" Phoenix was confused.

"She's Asian-American. Age: 25. 171 pounds. Eye color: ocean blue." Russell paused. "The best shade of blue you'll see on anybody."

"Wait, the best?" Phoenix said.

"It's a rare eye color." Phoenix is bitter as Russell isn't giving in to her emotions. "She's been in the organization for two years and recently got promoted to elite privileges, but this isn't an ordinary elite."

"What makes you say that?" Darrell said.

"She's been trained into acrobatics, but she's a rōnin."

"What the hell is a rōnin?" Phoenix said.

"A person who trains without the majority of assistance from a master in Japanese beliefs. She mostly taught herself, but she did get assistance. There's a section in the organization that goes outside from ballistics and firearms. The organization doesn't hold people from only the United States. The people can range from different countries, too. We all know that the organization is huge in diversity, that's why the melting pot is called the International Foundation for Human Resources."

"Oh, this should be interesting," Phoenix said, cracking her knuckles.

"She specializes in blades. She carries platinum grade katanas that are capable of making clean cuts into the skin and can deliver critical damage to the bones if you let it."

"So, what are we facing up against this time?"

"As far as I know, there's not that much activity coming from other agents. She's currently the lone wolf in her situation. She'll be hiding out in Miami, Florida. However, her details and whereabouts are unknown, though."

"What goes on? Is the organization just one disorganized community of people with a different backstory to them?" Darrell said.

"Theoretically, yes. Rose wasn't much of a talker from when she came in, but she got around, though. Nobody really seemed to bother her. She was an immediate acceptance, she fit right in. It didn't take much for people to notice her, but it wasn't because of her physical traits, but because of where she came from and what she's been through. Let's just say

that."

"So, what kind of weapons do we need?" Phoenix said.

"Your usual ones, of course. I'll be typing away and doing

some research for a while. Why don't you guys improvise?

That might help with our next mission. I'll be coming with you

guys."

"Alright."

Darrell and Phoenix walk out of the computer room and

head into the garage. They notice Adrian looking at the

Lamborghini. He places his hands on his hips with a silver

wrench in his hands. "I don't know how these people do it

sometimes," Adrian said aloud.

"What do you mean?" Phoenix said as she and Darrell

walk up to him.

"The vehicles, the killing, the weapons, you name it."

"We're going after an Asian-American this time. Name's

Rose Takeuchi. She's hiding out in Miami, Florida." Adrian

pauses in shock as he drops his wrench, "Takeuchi, you said?"

"Yes, wouldn't lie about that, would we?" Adrian walks up to them, "I would watch out for her." Darrell was getting concerned, "Why, what would make her so dangerous?"

"It's not the danger factor you need to be worried about, it's her backstory."

"What's in her backstory since Russell didn't tell us her whole background?" Phoenix said. Adrian takes a deep breath, "Well, I'm pretty sure that Russell told you that everyone has a reason to get in the organization."

"We were already notified that."

"Getting applied in the organization comes in two ways, the easy way or the hard way. Well, to them, it's easy. Like the previous conspiracy leaks, if you sometimes see people in black appearing in business attire, you're going to be captured."

"So, what does this have to do with Rose?" Phoenix said. Adrian sighs again, "She had a great family and lived a comfortable life. That is until 2018, she was ambushed by IFHR. They shot her parents down and take her away."

Phoenix gasped, "That's terrible."

"She was taken into one of the many shitholes that they established and evaluated her. Russell and I have known each other a while during this time."

Adrian goes into one of his flashbacks from when he met Rose, "We were in a large training room." The room was white as there were many pieces of training equipment such as dumbbells and firing ranges. "Two agents pushed open the doors and let her go. They said to her, 'Go show them what you're made of.'" Rose slowly walked into the room. Everyone stared at her, even got out of their way for her. She wore a clear, red robe with sandals. "They took her to the other side of the room, where nobody ever went into. People were saying quietly, 'Why are they taking her in there?'"

The two agents open the door to reveal a large room with an assortment of different blades and knives. There was a window by the side of the door that almost extended through the side of the entire training room. There were targets that were separated evenly as parts of the room were dimly lit from the ceiling. The targets had the shape of human torsos. One of the agents walked by the sword stands by the side and picked up a black sheath. The agent handed the sword to Rose, "Platinum-grade, be careful."

Rose gently takes the sword and unsheathes it, revealing its reflective and smooth material. She looked down in despair at the blade to see her face. A tear runs down her eye and looked at the targets. She was breathing heavily from the emotions growing inside. She yells in agony and runs toward the targets. She sliced them with fluent accuracy as she brought them to pieces.

"Everyone was shocked by what they saw," Adrian said. "Everyone was talking about her as she was wielding that sword. The organization made sure that no one else knew about her. The agents grabbed her and pulled her away. They took her into the initiation room in the middle of her session. Russell looked at me and said, 'There's a new kid on the block.' We never saw her again since." The flashback ended.

"Wow," Phoenix said. "I guess people do have their backstories before getting in the organization."

"That's why people should never judge others for who they are and what they've been through. IFHR's broke many rules on that. Part of the multitude of reasons why I left there."

"I have a feeling that Russell likes her. He was hesitant when he brought her up. Pretty surprising for a guy that acts like a hard-ass on a daily basis," Phoenix said.

"Yeah, you'll get that with a guy like him. Well, I'm going to check out the vehicles for any problems. I have nothing else better to do."

"That's not necessarily true, Adrian."

"Well, I've always had childhood dreams of becoming a mechanic. At least the organization's decent at allowing you to select your position. Very rarely, though, they hardly give anybody a chance in there. Well, I'll be out here if you need me."

"Alright," Darrell said.

Darrell and Phoenix walk out of the garage and go back upstairs to meet with Russell. He got up from his computer and said, "So, you guys ready?"

"Yeah, we're ready," Phoenix said.

"Alright, you're going to need some rest for tomorrow. This will be the longest drive we ever took." Darrell and Phoenix turn around and start to walk out. "And, Phoenix, I have something for you." They turn around again and walk to Russell.

"Oh, you're going to be nice to me now?" Phoenix said.

"Come with me." Russell leads them to the cabinets beside the computers. He opens the top drawer to pull out a black leather suit with a zipper in the center of its chestal region. The suit came with a belt around the waist with straps around the chest and back. Phoenix was confused, "What's this for?"

"Well, since we're going after a female, some of the female agents wear these leather suits. Not just for style, but they help blend in with the darkness."

"Oh, then, I guess this should come in handy."

"You may need to bring the suit with you. You guys need your jackets, too. This one may be a special mission."

"Is it because it's a female?" Darrell said.

"No, like I said, there's a mystery behind everyone's life." Something popped up in Russell's mind, "Oh, and almost forgot, I need to get you set up with formal attire, Darrell."

"What kind of attire?" Darrell said.

"Just the basic colors. Black suit jacket, pants, shoes, and a white dress shirt. Don't forget the black tie." Russell opens the middle drawer and carefully pulls out the attire with a silver hanger keeping them neatly organized. "That's going to be your disguise." Darrell takes the attire, "And as for you?"

"Same as the last mission. She probably won't recognize me and think I'm Conway."

"Why did you go crazy back there, Russell? Is there something you're not telling us?" Phoenix said.

"I've been in the organization long enough to test my own sanity. After a while, we're going to have to get some rest."

"Alright, but what are you going to do?" Phoenix said.

"I'm probably going to be up all night. I'm going to do some research on this woman. She may be a lead to the other sections of the organization and how it all started."

"Okay. It's been a nice talk," Phoenix said reluctantly. "We're going to be hanging in the living room for most of the day."

"Alright, I'll be up here if you need me."

Darrell and Phoenix went downstairs and open the door to the living room. They lounge on the recliners and look at an assortment of fashion and automotive magazines for the remainder of the day.

As Darrell and Phoenix are sound asleep at night, Russell sits in the dark as the computers illuminate his face. He's still looking into the database of people working throughout IFHR. He looks at Rose's portrait and stares at it. He looks down in frustration and whispers, "Where the hell could you be, Rose?" He sighs and turns off the computers. "I should probably get some sleep." He slowly walks down the stairs and into his bedroom to get ready for the next mission.

Chapter 12: Aeromancer

August 11, 2020

Miami, Florida

The city of Miami was bright in the morning and filled with palm trees as the clear skies shined the streets. The group was driving by the ocean on the South Bayshore Drive. "Rose has a way of blending in, so, she has instinct," Russell said. "I would be careful and look for anything with a suit like you have, Phoenix." Darrell has his attire on.

"Where do you think she could be?" Phoenix said.

"I don't know. Probably somewhere where there's not a whole bunch of light. Look for places that have shadows, lots of them."

Rose is hiding in the dark entrance of a parking garage. She's wearing a black leather suit with two black sheathed platinum swords on her back. She's crouched down by a small stairwell to avoid being seen by the light from the streets in the distance. There was nobody coming from outside. She gets up and turns around to face the other side. She's heavily breathing as she's sprinting towards the street ahead of her, but is still inside the parking garage.

A couple agents walk beside the entrance from the other side and face Rose as she sees their silhouettes. They are armed with assault rifles. Rose was terrified. "Stay right where you are, Rose!" one of the agents said. "It'll be alright, you're just one moment away from home."

Rose looks down and sighs in despair and kneels as the agents slowly walk to her. One of the agents turns on a flashlight to shine it around and locate Rose. They spot Rose and shine the light on her. "Hey, it'll be okay," one of the agents said. "It'll all be over soon." The agent lets out his hand, "Come home with us."

Rose looks up at the agents and looks around. She looks at the agent talking to him and quickly unsheathes one of her swords. Without giving any reaction time, she stabs the agent through the diaphragm, causing him to gurgle loudly and widen his eyes. Rose stands up and yanks the sword out of him. The agent drops with his chest facing the ground with large amounts of blood coming out of him. She viciously looks at the agents beside her and slowly unsheathes her other sword. She charges at one of the agents and slashes deep incisions across his chest, cutting through the clothes and exposing his skin. She cuts into the side of the agent's neck, hitting his jugular vein as blood quickly squirts out. The agent gurgled and thudded to the ground, dying instantly.

Rose locks on the last agent standing, forming a shadow in front of him. She charges at him. He fires a bullet, but she deflects it with her swords. She slides with her knees on the ground, dodging another bullet. She slashes the agent's leg, yelling from the burn of the cut. He begins to kneel as Rose

gets up. She walks to him and viciously stabs him in his chest.

She grins and whispers as she gets close to his face, "I'm

already home!"

Rose pulls the sword out of the agent and runs for the

door behind her in the distance. She budges through the door

and runs through a well-lit narrow hallway with several pipes

and valves. She is hyperventilating while sprinting to the door

ahead of her. She grunts and fiercely pushes the door and

runs to the right to see the exit sign above another door. She

budges through the door to see the cityscape around her. She

looks around to spot her vehicle parked on a sidewalk, which

is a white Scion coupe. The vehicle was in a moderate class.

She ran to the vehicle and drove into the streets.

"She could be anywhere. Where could she be?" Russell

said as the group was exiting the bay area. They were going

straight as there are tall buildings and moderately dense

traffic. "Now watch your surroundings. Agents could be hiding anywhere. They're going to be on high alert, especially if they're roaming around in her hometown."

"How long has she been out of the organization?" Phoenix said.

"Hard to say, hard to tell, but backing out in IFHR is a big restriction. Once the initiation process is complete, you're permanently one of them. They would track you down even if you give no effort."

"How did you get out so easily?"

"Pfff! Assholes didn't know what hit 'em. They pissed me off the whole time I was there. Had enough of their shit, so I decided to retaliate."

"What was the deal with you and Abrams?"

"Abrams, just another sorry bastard that roamed in the herd. Him and I didn't get along real well. Thought he wanted to be the tough guy in the crew, but realized he messed with the wrong person. He didn't even see it coming. He got what he deserved."

"Sliced his neck up real good. Goddamn," Darrell said.

"I sensed that your rage was getting out of hand back there," Phoenix said.

"Rage is the only thing I know when it comes to that shithole," Russell said. They slow down as they approach a red traffic light. "Don't go speeding, we still have to follow the rules of the road," Russell said.

"Well, no shit, we're citizens," Phoenix said.

"The organization uses the outside world to their advantage to blend in," Russell said. They drive at cruising speed as the light turns green. "Virtually every city in the United States and almost every other nation are in the level of prosperity. Since the world is in a cleaner status and more economically established, that was the perfect recipe for IFHR's strategy leading to their cover-up and demise. That was only the beginning of its establishment. Many conspiracy theorists state that the current president was involved with covering the organization's activity."

Darrell and Phoenix were in shock and looked at each other. Darrell said, "The president?"

"Yes, even President Donovan Lavensa was a popular topic in the stir of the conspiracy," Russell said.

"But, how could he be involved? He's done so much for this country," Darrell said.

"He was able to bring the poverty level down to almost a 1% rate for a nation of about three hundred and fifty million. He's a good president, but some people say that he's the founder."

The group stops in front of a red traffic light. They see the white Scion from their right. They were not on the same road. "Keep an eye on the Scion, that could be Rose," Russell said. Russell looks on the driver's side to see that it's her, stopping at a traffic light.

Rose panics and speeds off going straight, cutting off several drivers as they beep their horns. "Don't move a muscle!" Russell said. They see two supercars zipping through the road, heading towards the same direction as Rose. "Shit!"

Russell said. "Follow them, NOW!" The group floors the

throttle and drifts to follow the supercars. "Come on, step on

it! Let's go!" The group accelerates as the vehicles make their

bodies feel lighter. The supercars were still distant as the

group makes their way into second gear. They quickly shift

lanes to avoid collisions and catch up to the supercars.

The group fires at the supercars, making small dents on

their rear bumpers. They were in the moderate class. As the

group drives through a city block, they notice two infantry

vehicles from Base 00519 coming from both sides behind

them. "Shit!" Phoenix said.

"Damn it, there may be more that's coming to us!"

Darrell said.

Darrell and Russell shoot the supercars' tires. The

infantry vehicles accelerate closer to the group. Russell

activates the shotgun and fires at one of the infantry vehicles.

It did damage, but no significance. The infantry vehicle's front bumper was severely damaged, but no penetration.

Russell shot a few more rounds and penetrated through the front on both sides. The penetration was big enough to pierce through the interior, killing the agents inside. The vehicle began to slow down.

Darrell activated the machine guns and turned on the magnetism. He activated the armor piercing rounds and fired at the infantry vehicle. The bullets pierced through the metal as they cut through the agents.

Rose was drifting into another city block in the distance. "Turn right before we lose her!" Russell said. The group arrives at the block Rose entered in.

As the group drove through the block, they notice two tanks coming from one side. Phoenix gasped, "SHIT! STOP THE CAR!" Darrell pressed hard on the brake, but Russell continued on. One of the tanks moved their turret to Russell and Rose. The tank fired a large, propelled missile at a building, destroying the glass windows and obliterating its interior. The blast claimed a few lives of the people close to the impact. The people surrounding it ran and yelled in panic and fear.

Darrell and Phoenix panic as the tanks move further out, close to the middle of the road. "Darrell, what the hell are you doing?! FUCKING DRIVE!" Phoenix yells.

Darrell slams the throttle and drives toward the tanks. The tanks' turrets follow his vehicle as he drifts away from them. While drifting, the tanks lower their turrets and fire at the road, missing Darrell by a few feet. The blast left a hole in the road as it blew up a few commuters. Darrell slams the throttle again and drives away from the tanks. "Phoenix, watch the tanks!" Darrell said. She looks in her side mirror, "They're driving towards us!"

Darrell continues to accelerate as he's weaving around traffic. The tanks fire from the distance, barely missing Darrell. "We have to lose them!" Phoenix said.

"Well, no shit!" Darrell yelled.

As the Lamborghini was increasing speed, Darrell stops

and drifts to the right. He drifts again to see the sun shine

down on the streets. "Did you lose them?" Russell said.

"For now, we did. Shit, that was close!" Darrell said.

"Where are you at right now?" Phoenix said.

"Far away from where you're at," Russell said.

"Just tell us where you're at!" Phoenix yelled.

"I can't do that right now, you need to find someplace

safe to where they can't find you!" Russell said.

"What the hell do you mean you can't?! We're on a

mission!"

"Just do as I fucking say, damn it! It's not worth the risk!

Just find somewhere safe!"

Darrell accelerates and enters an unaffected street, "He's

right, Phoenix. Our vehicles are pretty much useless against

the tanks. We need to hide for right now. It may take until it

approaches night." Darrell drives around the city to

eventually find a place to hide from the tanks.

Chapter 13: Pursuit

The day later turned to night as the skies projected the stars. The skies were in an obsidian and dark blue texture, indicating that dawn is close. Darrell and Phoenix are sitting in the Lamborghini in an entrance of a parking lot next to a grassy plain. The vehicle was completely shut off as they were hiding under the large shadow of a tall building from the side. "What the hell is Russell doing?" Darrell said.

"I still don't trust him. Have you noticed that he's tried to avoid us almost every time?" Phoenix said.

"I have noticed that a little bit."

"Maybe Rose isn't what we think, from what Adrian said."

"Not everybody in the organization wanted to get initiated."

"She reminds me of my husband." Phoenix looks down and sighs.

"They killed her family without her even expecting it," Darrell said.

"She didn't deserve it. Even though we don't know her, there could be something that Russell's not telling us."

Darrell looks down and thinks, "How the fuck did we get in this mess in the first place?"

"That's what I keep asking myself. Every day, every night."

"I should've listened to the conspiracy, my life wouldn't have been this difficult if this existed."

"I should've listened, too, but you should be grateful that I saved your life that day."

"I am, I'm just saying. My life would be better off if I only believed in it. If only I knew about what they wore. The answer was right in front of me this whole time. I was too damn stupid enough to not see it."

Darrell and Phoenix hear loud engine sounds whistling from the distance. Darrell was about to turn on the vehicle, but Phoenix stopped him by grabbing his arm. "Shh, don't start the vehicle!" Phoenix whispers. They notice Rose's and Russell's vehicles driving by at an alarming speed. They don't see Darrell and Phoenix. They both take a closer look at Rose's vehicle. Rose seemed to be scared and frightened. They see Rose and Russell keep straight until they turn and disappear from their sight. "Go after them, NOW!" Phoenix yells.

Darrell starts the vehicle and turns into the direction of Rose and Russell, propelling through first gear. "I never should've trusted him," Phoenix said, cocking her pistol. "What the hell is he doing?"

"I guess we'll find out, apparently they don't have a

schedule to follow by." They roam in the city's infrastructure

and resume the pursuit.

Chapter 14: Arma

August 12, 2020

It approaches day as the group pursues Rose and overtakes the commuters ahead of them. "They should be coming any minute!" Phoenix said.

Two armored Chevrolet pickup trucks pull out in front of the group and get behind Rose. The group accelerates closer to the trucks as they heard their loud and boisterous engines. They switch lanes to drive beside the trucks. Darrell presses the horseshoe magnet button and readies the pulse system. The screen reads as N as the vehicle beside him was in the same pole. He set the power to 10%. The pulse slightly pushed the truck away, but it quickly recovered.

Darrell raises the power to 20%. The truck beside him attempted to ram him, but he accelerated out of the way just in time before the action was executed. The truck turned onto the lane Darrell was in. There was an open lane between the trucks. He turned in that lane and slowed down until he was in between the trucks. "Darrell, what are you doing?" Russell said.

"You better watch out," Darrell said. Russell realized he activated the pulse system and slowed down to keep his distance.

Darrell holds the horseshoe button until it glows and presses it again. The pulse creates a sound of an electronic circuit and fiercely pushes the trucks away from each other. The force was so strong that one of the trucks hit the wall of a building with punishing force, totaling the vehicle. The other truck spun out of control, causing it to almost tip over. It stopped spinning as it came in contact with a bridge support

on its side with devastating consequences, killing the agents
by fracturing their skulls.

"Damn!" Darrell said, looking at the damage of the
trucks. They drift into a road covered with sunlight as the
group follows Rose. "Stay focused. She could be heading
anywhere," Russell said.

As the group keeps driving straight, two armored tanks
and a small fleet of armored infantry vehicles unexpectedly
come out from both sides and pursue them. The tanks are
painted black with a metallic finish and heavily modified
aesthetics on the exterior. The tanks were accelerating quickly
as they have a claimed top speed of a hundred and twenty
miles per hour, around two and a half times faster than a
Type 99 tank. The tanks were about ten feet tall with turrets
that could fit a seven hundred millimeter projectile. Darrell
looks in the rear-view mirror, "Those can't be ordinary tanks."

"Those are Armas! Elite tanks! IFHR's resort for
emergency ops!" Russell said. The infantry vehicles move

around the tanks and accelerate towards the group. The tanks

plow through a couple commuters and run them over as their

dual tracks crushed them to half their size. They lock their

aim at the ground, closely aiming at Darrell and Russell. They

fire high-powered artillery shots at the ground, missing

Darrell and Russell by mere feet. They swerve away from the

direction of the blast. "Best get our asses moving unless you

want to be IFHR's scrap metal!" Russell said. The damage left

small craters in the ground, blasting the surrounding vehicles

out of sight.

The group pushes their vehicles with brutal acceleration.

The infantry vehicles fire bursts of machine guns at the group

as the tanks aim their turrets at the buildings on both sides.

The tanks were losing distance as they couldn't keep up with

the speed of the group. They fire the artillery at the bottom

of one of the buildings in the distance of where the group is

driving. The impact spreads in the building as it explodes and

almost takes it off of its support.

The group hears the building rustle down as they see it slowly timber. Phoenix panicked, "Darrell, you better go!" The infantry vehicles are still behind them. The building falls and collapses, obstructing the commuters' sight surrounding it. "Did we lose the tanks?" Phoenix said, looking behind her. Darrell looks in the rear-view mirror.

The building's being chipped away in large chunks as it's accompanied by explosions, creating a large cloud of smoke. The tanks plow through the building's rubble unscathed. "Hell, no!" Darrell said.

The tanks fire at the group from the distance. The artillery shots were both heading towards Darrell. "Goddamnit!" he yelled. The shots missed him as they flew just above him. They were moving towards a tall and wide glass building in the distance. The shots ripped through it as the first floor collapsed to the ground. The building started to slowly tip over, but was moving slower than the other one. The building was falling towards the group.

The group notices Rose activating her nitrous system in front of them as they heard her vehicle. They see small cyan colored flames coming from her exhausts. Her vehicle propelled to blistering speed. "What the hell is she doing?" Phoenix said. As the building was still tipping over, Rose continued to drive towards the direction of the falling building. She drives into the building as the floor became a ramp. "What the-?!" Darrell was shocked.

"Activate your nitrous, we're going in the building," Russell said.

Phoenix was shocked and yelled, "What?! Are you crazy, Russell?! It's collapsi-"

"Just FUCKING do it, we need to go after her!"

Darrell firmly looks at Phoenix, "Hang on." He looks down and activates the nitrous system as Russell does the same. Darrell and Phoenix are forced onto their seats as the vehicle accelerates at rapid levels. The infantry vehicles activate their nitrous, but the group doesn't notice. Darrell and Russell enter the falling building as most of the infantry vehicles move out of the way except for a couple that follow them.

The ceiling lights in the building break as its incline is gradually increasing. The group sees Rose nearing the exit and turn to the left. The infantry vehicles turn to Rose's direction and pursue her instead.

Rose drives out of the building and disappears. "ROSE!" Russell yelled. The group exits the building and fly through the air. Their engines were revving to their highest before they let go of the throttle. They panicked as they were a few hundred feet in the air. "HOLY SHIT!" Darrell said, looking down at the ground. He notices the infantry vehicles following Rose on another city block.

The group looks ahead and see a building's roof just below them. They both slam the brakes as they land. Their tires screech and create clouds of smoke until they approach the center of its roof. They all got out and get into an argument. Phoenix walks up to Russell, "NOW what do we do, Russell?!" She pushes him, causing him to stumble backward.

"Relax!" Russell said. She pushes him again.

"Phoenix, stop! He's going to fall off the roof!" Darrell yelled. She pushes him again until he's at the edge of the roof. Russell grabs her arms. "RELAX!" Russell yells. He pushes her until she tumbles and falls. Darrell runs up to her and lets his arm out. She grabs his arm as he pulls her up. "Thanks, Darrell," Phoenix said.

She walks up to Russell again, but this time, she isn't physically hostile. "So, what do we do, Russell?" she says calmly, but is still angry. Russell looks down to the ground to see the building beside them turned into rubble. He walks away from the edge, "We have to think of a plan. We have to get back on ground level somehow." They negotiate as they face a new obstacle, the various heights of the buildings surrounding them.

Chapter 15: Rooftops

"So, what's the plan?" Phoenix said, frustrated. Russell

looks around, "Well, first off, we have to find a way to lower

ground. Every city has a pattern of heights of some sort." He

looks around and locks his sight onto the building by

Phoenix's side. "See that building over there?" Phoenix

looked in Russell's point of view. "That building's roof is lower

than this one. The roof we're on is wide enough for us to

drive on. We need to get a head start in order to pull this off

in one shot."

"How far apart is the building from this one?" Darrell

said. Russell walks past Phoenix and looks at the building ahead of him. Russell looks down towards the road, "Maybe fifty feet. I would get a head start right now. We can't stay up here forever."

As the group walks to their vehicles, they notice the two tanks from earlier coming from the distance. "Oh, shit," Darrell said quietly to himself.

"That means now, we gotta act fast!" Russell said. They get in their vehicles and set them in reverse. They turn and back up until they are aligned towards the building ahead of them. "Don't know what they're planning, but this might not end well," Russell said.

Russell notices the tanks moving their turrets at the building they're on. He panics, "Shit, they saw us! Go now, they're going to blow up the building!"

The group accelerates and drive to the building ahead of them. As they drove off of the roof, the building collapses as it was impacted by one of the artillery shots and a loud boom.

Phoenix looked back on the damage and panicked, "Shit, that was close!"

"I'm not looking back!" Darrell said. They just made it onto another building. The tanks were just turning to their direction, keeping their distance. Phoenix looks behind her, "They're following us!" The group keeps accelerating as they reach the end of the building. The tanks shoot at the edge of the top of the building as the artillery almost hits the group's vehicles. They just drove over the roof as the blast blew a hole through the targeted shot. Phoenix panicked, "Shit, that was close!"

The group lands on another building that's about fifty feet from the ground. "Hang on!" Darrell said. They drive over a slanted ramp ahead of them and go through the air. One of the tanks shoot at the building while the other shoots near Darrell, barely missing him. The shot blows another hole in the center of a building ahead of them. They land on the ground as their vehicles create small showers of sparks.

"Where the hell's Rose?!" Russell said.

"Couldn't find her!" Phoenix said.

"We have to find her quickly!" Phoenix was thinking and said, "Wait a minute, why do you want her so badly?" Russell hesitated and sighed, "Because that's somebody I care about." They drift into another city block and resume the pursuit after Rose.

Chapter 16: Rōnin

Rose was hiding on the fifth floor of a parking garage with dim, beige lighting. She was crouched down beside a light on a wall. The floors are large and wide as the sun was shining down on the floor in the distance. She heard footsteps from the distance as they were coming from the entrance of the floor. She slowly unsheathed one of her swords to prepare herself. An agent shows up with a flashlight. He walks and looks around to find Phoenix. "Rose?" the agent yells. He turns away from the direction of Rose and looks around as he sees the sun shine down on the floor. Rose stands up and sprints to the opposite side the agent came in, which was the exit. Her footsteps were loud enough for the agent to hear them. She laid and slid down the slant until she was on flat ground. The agent was startled and shined the light towards where Rose went. She heard him draw his pistol. She gets up and stands behind a wall and slowly walks up the stairs beside the slant. She heard footsteps getting louder as he was coming closer. "Rose, are you there?" he yelled.

As Rose walks towards the end of the stairs, she crouches down and readies her sword. The agent walks towards the wall and says, "Rose?"

Rose peeks out in surprise and quickly slashes him in the foot. The agent yells from the burning of the cut. She quickly gets up and walks toward the agent with an angered look. The agent grunts as he fires a round at Rose, but she quickly deflects it, causing it to ricochet to the other side. She walks closer to him as he walks backward, limping from his foot.

Rose slashes him in the chest and arms, causing him to fall to the ground. She charges and crouches on him, pinning him down. She raises her sword and stabs him in the diaphragm, execution style. The agent's head starts to redden as he grunts from the pain. Blood comes out of his mouth as he gurgles from the wounds. He gives in to the pain and dies as Rose shows no remorse. She gets up and quickly pulls the sword out of his chest.

Rose heard a series of footsteps as she walks away from the dead agent. Five agents were coming from the entrance. All of them were wearing thick, leather outfits with the white IFHR insignia in the middle of their chests. They were also wearing thin, clear helmets around their heads as the back of them were solid gray. There was one agent that was dressed differently, which is one of the agents that took her in the training room. He was standing in the middle and is the only one solely wearing business attire.

The agent is Miles Fabian. He's been involved with IFHR

for two years and is twenty-seven years old. He has short brown hair and white skin color. "Ready your weapons, go after her," Miles said. "I see that you've been busy," Rose said. The four agents run up to Rose, surrounding her and raise their swords. "Alright, let her have it," Miles said.

Rose looks at all four agents. She crouches down and kicks one of them, making him lose balance. She slashes him in the kneecap and punches a hole through the glass part of his helmet. She gets up and knees him in the face and cuts a hole through the center of his head, killing him instantly. One of the agents charges after her and swings his sword. Rose and the agent are dueling as their swords are clanging feverishly. They stop swinging their swords as both of them block each other, forming an X. They're both pushing each other as they are trying to break free from their blocks.

Rose spins her sword around to break free. She hears the footsteps of another agent come from behind. She looks back to see the agent as he charges. She looks away and sees the other agent swing his sword towards her. Rose does a quick spin and moves out of the way just in time before the agent could make his move. The agent behind her misses and almost hits the agent in front of him. Rose goes behind one of the agents and elbows him hard in the back of the head. As an agent is about to turn around, she makes a swift kick in the back of his leg, temporarily stunning him. He kneels to the ground. Rose takes her sword and cuts a hole through his chest, killing him.

Rose charges after the remaining agents. Both of the agents swing their swords at the same time. Rose blocks both of them, but she's not able to break free. The agents apply more pressure with their swords, making it harder for Rose to stand up. This caused her to kneel to the ground. She was panicking as she was looking for a solution to break free. She focuses on the agents' legs.

Rose takes a deep breath and trips one of the agents, making him drop his sword. She moves her sword up and breaks free from the other agent. She stands up and charges

at them. She kicks one of the agents in the side and stabs him

in the chest. She heard the last agent come from behind. She

looks back and kicks him in the chest, causing him to move

back a couple steps. She turns around and walks to the agent.

The agent walks to her and swings his sword, but she blocks

it. She jumps in the air and kicks him in the head, shattering

the front of his helmet, pushing him backward. He walks to

Rose again and swings his sword. She blocks it again and

swings it to the side with no effort. She quickly slashes the

agent in the chest. Rose stops moving. The agent kneels to

the ground and stares at her. She walks up to the agent and

executes him by cutting through his head. She breathes

heavily and expresses anger. She puts her foot on the agent's

chest and pushes him, pulling the sword out.

Rose walks up to Miles in anger. He looks at the dead

bodies behind her as he has his arms crossed. "So, I see that

you have been gaining some experience over the past years,"

Miles said.

"I didn't have anybody to teach me. I can take care of myself," Rose said.

"How does it feel to get what you want?"

"You don't even know how it feels," Rose said. They start walking around in circles as they look at each other menacingly. "You killed my family. You invaded my hometown. There's nothing that will repay that after what you did to me. Why me? Why choose me? What makes me so special against all others?"

"We needed a recruit, that's how the organization goes. They go in for the kill and take the prey. That's how it is in the animal kingdom. That's how Barrett did the job, snatched Phoenix's knight in shining armor. It was the perfect opportunity, kind of like your situation. Now, isn't that interesting?" Miles laughs with no remorse.

"She wasn't even a target, until you decided to let the organization take each other's lives. Pretty sick-minded business you operate on a daily basis."

"Darrell was the main target in the situation. Phoenix was the bait. The war has only begun, so, you better be prepared." Rose was getting infuriated, "I fight my own war. Stay out of it!"

"I'd hate to break the news for you, but this doesn't involve you. These are two different events that are taking place all at once. We killed your family, but that's too bad for you." They stop walking. "Hmm, let me think." Miles points his finger up, "Oh, that's right, you've been initiated! You're automatically one of us, and there's nothing you can do about it! And turning your back on us. That's a big no-no in the organization. The punishment is at its highest level when you break those rules."

"I have my reasons to."

Miles slowly pulls out both of his swords one by one, "So, what's going through your head right now? Fearful, scared, or is it revenge that you're looking for?"

"I only know vengeance now, after the coming days. I've

been waiting for the perfect moment to avenge my family."

"Then, what are you WAITING FOR?! COME AFTER ME!"

"I don't thirst for blood. Unlike you, I don't take lives just for the fun of it." Miles says menacingly, "Well, in the organization, we don't work together. We don't make amends, we fight to the death."

Rose slowly unsheathes her other sword, holding both swords, "Then make your move."

Miles and Rose charge at each other and swing their swords around each other. They continuously block and apply force to each other. "Have you considered going back to basic training?!" Miles taunted.

"*Tst,* I didn't need training." Rose breaks free, but Miles charges at her again. She blocks him again, but she's pinned down. "Remember that time when we killed your family?!" Miles taunted. Rose was getting enraged. "Aw, are you going to cry now?! Maybe you should've stayed home where you belong, with us!"

Rose breaks free and charges at Miles. They swing their swords around and continue to block each other. Rose counter strikes Miles, causing him to expose his chest. She slides down and slashes his leg. Miles grunts from the pain and is temporarily stunned.

Rose walks up to Miles. He looks up at her and says, "Go ahead, kill me, you're only going to make things worse for yourself." She raises her blades and hesitates. She breathes heavily, thinking about the events leading to her family's death. She lets her swords down, "You know what? Even though you killed my family, nothing will change that. You scarred me forever." She walks around Miles until she's behind his back. "But that doesn't matter." She stabs through Miles' back as he sees the platinum blade go through him. "That doesn't mean I'm not going to avenge my family." She pushes the sword in further, causing Miles to gurgle. "I'm a rōnin. You should've learned that by now. You should've thought twice before you decided to turn my home into a slaughterhouse!" She quickly pulls the sword out of Miles as his face reddens and loudly gurgles. She places one of her swords around his neck. "This is my last mission." She bends down and talks to him, "But before I finish the mission, let me make this clear right now." She slowly talks in his ear, "Those who live by the blade, die by the blade!" She slices Miles' throat as blood spills out of his neck like a fountain. Bloods spills on Rose's face. He collapses to the ground as blood spreads around the center of his body.

Rose stands up and slowly sheathed her swords behind her back. She turns around and runs toward the floor entrance. She vaults over the railing and jumps down the stairs and sprints. She eventually reaches the first floor to find her Scion. She gets in her vehicle and propels out of the parking garage.

Rose drifts onto the road and accelerates. She wasn't scared as she was brazen. She propels onward as the engine screams, engaging in pursuit.

Chapter 17: The Warrior Within

The group scours through the city blocks to find Rose.

They see a small fleet of infantry vehicles and Arma tanks

turning in the distance, but didn't see Rose. "She couldn't

have gone far," Russell said. They accelerate and drift towards

the direction of the tanks, following them. "She should be

close," Phoenix said. The group was far away from the parking

garage Rose exited. The tanks quickly move their turrets and

aim at the group. The group quickly swerve around the

turrets' aim. The tanks fire shots at a cluster of commuters,

barely missing Darrell and Russell.

The group accelerates past the fleet until they are behind the infantry vehicles and tanks. They fire at the infantry vehicles with their rear machine guns, cutting through their armor. The tanks run over the infantry vehicles and flattens them like a pancake. They notice a car speeding and drifting in the distance behind them and going towards the tanks. Russell looks in his rear-view mirror, "Wait a second, is that Rose?!" The tanks aim their turrets at Rose as she's coming closer. "Oh, shit, they're going to shoot her!" Darrell said.

Rose weaves in both directions as the tanks barely miss her. She accelerates in between the tanks and the group. She accelerates further as she weaves through a dense block of city traffic. The tanks fire just above the group, causing them to jump in their seats. Phoenix gasps. "What's wrong?" Darrell said.

"They're going to hit Rose!" Phoenix panicked.

The artillery instead impacts buildings on both sides. The shots blasted the first couple floors of the buildings. "We have to get through!" Russell said.

"What?! Are you crazy?!" Phoenix yelled.

"Just FUCKING DO IT!"

The tanks continue firing at other buildings in the distance as the group enters another city block. Their bodies tense up as the buildings slowly collapse between them.

"Step on it, keep moving!" Russell said. They keep accelerating as they narrowly escape as the buildings collapsed behind them. The tanks fire two more shots before they get crushed and buried under the rubble.

The group sees the shots going towards a dense section of the oncoming road as Rose was beside it. Russell gasps and yells, "NO!" The shots exploded as they incinerated the oncoming vehicles. The shock wave was powerful enough to make Rose tip over to her side. Due to the high rate of speed, she enters a series of unforgiving barrel rolls. The glass inside her vehicle shattered as the shards cut into parts of her face.

The barrel rolls stop as the vehicle is on its wheelbase.

Rose's Scion was severely damaged. "Stop!" Russell said. The group slams on their brakes. They get out and sprint to Rose's aid. Rose climbs out of the vehicle with no problem while sustaining minor injuries across her body. She grunts from the cuts by the glass shards. Russell lets his arm out, "Rose!"

Suddenly, Rose hears the horn of a semi truck coming towards her way. She turns around and gasps as the semi does not slow down. Without giving any reaction, the semi bashes her vehicle, including Rose. Her vehicle pushes her with brute force, breaking her legs, almost damaging her diaphragm. She thuds hard to the ground, paralyzed from the impact. She coughs out blood as the semi screeched on its brakes. "Stop!" Russell said, yelling at the truck driver. The semi came to a full stop. "Alright, come on, let's go!"

The group goes around the semi as the truck driver comes out. "Oh, shit! Rose!" Russell said. They stop running and crouch down near Rose. The truck driver panics, "Ma'am, are you okay?!" Phoenix turns around, "Get going, sir!"

"Is there anything I can do to he-"

"Sir, go, it's best if you let us do it. Trust me, we got it from here." The truck driver walks to the group, "Well, I'm going to help anyway whether you like it or n-" Russell quickly gets up and points a pistol to his forehead with anger. He breathes heavily and says, "Go!" The truck driver slowly backs up to the semi as he panics and drives off.

The group refocuses their attention on Rose. "Rose, what's going on?" Phoenix said. Rose slowly turns her head to look at Phoenix. Her voice is weak, "..............Phoenix, ...is that............. you?" Phoenix was shocked, "Yes, how do you know my name?"

"...............And Darrell...., too."

"What's happening, Rose? Please talk to me."

"......I don't..... know...... how you guys..... did it, ...but you...... guys are.... lucky.... to be standing....... to this day."

"What are we facing up against, Rose?" Darrell said.

"Everybody..... knows..... about you.... in the.....

organization. You guys.... are on.... the top of their list."

"We know that for sure, we've killed many of them, but they still keep coming," Russell said. Rose looks at Russell in anger, "They... do.... nothing.... but.... kill.... people......, even... each other. They..... play it.... as a...... bloodsport. Tell... me... something I don't..... know." She looks at Phoenix and Darrell, "You can't... trust... them at... all. Don't... let them... trick you."

"So. what's next for us?" Phoenix said.

"They're planning something....... on a global... scale. How do... you think.... the "I"...... got..... in.... the organization's... NAME!" Rose grunts from the pain and coughs again as blood comes out of her mouth. Her body temporarily stops her from talking due to the damage around and inside her body. Phoenix gets close to her and gently places her hand on her diaphragm. Phoenix looks at Darrell and Russell in disgust, "Don't just sit there, fucking help her, she's dying!" They get close to Rose and place their hands on her stomach. Phoenix says quietly to Rose, "Just take a deep breath, it'll be okay." Phoenix brushes Rose's hair as she gives Rose instructions. "Breathe with me, okay?" Rose and Phoenix both take deep breaths. "There you go, that's it. Let's try this again, what's going on?"

"The organization... is going to... unleash devastation on.. the world... very soon. And they'll... win... if nobody tries... to stop them. So.. many.... have tried... to get out... of the organization... alive, but.... very few.... succeeded."

"But we can help you, Rose. You still have a chance to be free again! Just please, let us help you!" Phoenix attempts to grab Rose and pick her up, but Rose stops her by grabbing her arm. "No," Rose said.

Phoenix begins to cry in melancholy, "No? Why no? I lost my husband and that's devastating enough! I can't let somebody die in my arms again! I can't do that!"

Rose begins to cry, "Phoenix......., I am... so sorry... about your loss. You and I.... have crossed.. the same roads. My family.... was killed.... when they forced me... into the organization.

Phoenix couldn't handle all of the emotions going through her, "That is so horrible, Rose! How do you deal with that every day?!"

"It eats... me alive.... on the inside. I couldn't look... at myself... since that happened." Phoenix thinks about the day Warren died in her arms.

"But you don't have to pay for what happened, it's not your fault! You need to be free, Rose! We can help you!"

"Phoenix......, listen to me. I am.... free. My family's... waiting for me. This is my chance.... to feel.... redemption again." Phoenix cries profusely, "Please, no!"

"You.... and Darrell... may be humanity's only hope. It'll be okay....., Phoenix. Stay strong.... for us...., please. Do this... for your husband."

"I'm already living up to that promise."

"Here...., let me give you something..... before I go." Rose grunts from the pain in her arms as she slowly unsheathed her two swords from her back. She sets them on the ground beside her. "Take these swords. They can cut... through almost anything they're.. guarding themselves with." Phoenix slowly picks up swords and sees her face in them, "Did they give you these swords?"

"Use them.... wisely. There's always a tale... to pass down.... when it comes... to a rōnin." Phoenix chuckles to herself, "What do you mean by a rōnin?"

"They require no master. They mostly.... teach themselves...., let's just say that. I want... to tell you one more thing..... before I go." Phoenix moves closer to Rose. "You.... and Darrell.... can do this. But remember this....., Phoenix." Rose's voice gets more delayed, "Those.............. who live............ by the blade.............., die......... by the blade." Rose takes one more deep breath as her eyes remain open and dies peacefully.

Phoenix lays her head down on Rose's stomach and

wails. "Goddamnit!" she quickly gets up as Darrell and Russell do the same. Phoenix looks at Russell in disgust and shakes her head, "This is all your fault."

"Phoenix, calm dow-" Darrell was interrupted.

"This is ALL YOUR FAULT!" Phoenix pushes Russell and grabs him. Russell takes Phoenix and forcefully pushes her against the wall of a building, making her fall to the ground. Darrell gasps and runs to her aid, "Phoenix, are you okay?" He takes her arm and pulls her up.

"You sicken me!" Phoenix said to Russell. "Pushing a woman like that. *Tst*, you oughta stay in a prison cell."

"Calm down, Phoenix. Emotions are not going to make the situation any better," Russell said.

"Hmm, like you always tell me, is to calm down." Phoenix picks up Rose's swords as the group walks to their vehicles. "Oh, and Darrell, I just love how you don't show YOUR emotions most of the time besides for yourself."

The group gets in their vehicles and head out of Miami.

Phoenix looks at her reflection on the swords, "Wow, would you look at that? Another one that suffered like I did." She takes a deep breath. "I guess agents do have a story behind them."

Chapter 18: Negotiation

August 15, 2020

Downtown Los Angeles, California

Darrell, Phoenix, and Russell are discussing the events leading to Rose in the abandoned auto shop. They wore casual clothing and were all in the kitchen as they were standing. "You wanna tell me why you were yelling out her name?" Phoenix said to Russell. Russell hesitated, "I really don't know how to tell you."

"Well, I don't accept that answer, there has to be a reason!" Phoenix paused, "Wait a minute. Was she your love interest?" Russell looks down in despair, "Yes, she was."

"She was, huh? Apparently, you didn't show much

affection back at Miami!"

Phoenix noticed that Russell began to shed a tear and walks up to him, but not in sympathy, "Aw, are you crying?" Russell looks up. "Now you're going to start showing your emotions? But, you're one moment too late." She gets angry and yells, "How do think she's going to think of you after that?! You failed to protect her!" She pushes Russell onto the counter top on the side, "YOU FAILED HER! If you loved her, you should've brought her with you along with Adrian!" She briefly paused. "Boy, if I ever had the power to turn back time, I would've saved my damn husband instead of feeling sorry for myself! I have no sympathy for you crying."

"Didn't you hear what she said?! The whole world's going to be involved!" Russell yelled. Phoenix takes a coffee mug behind her and throws it at the cupboard and says, "Forget about your fucking missions! It always has to be revolved around you, doesn't it?! I still don't trust you because how do I know? I've noticed that every time you come with us, you brought us into nothing but trouble."

Darrell joins, "Really, Phoenix? Without him, we wouldn't have stood a chance against them!" Suddenly, something came up in Russell's head, "Guys, we can't stay here tomorrow. We have to get moving by dawn."

"Alright, you know what? I'm done with you, Russell. It's not my damn fault that you got in the organization in the first place," Phoenix said.

"Even if I tried to back out, that wouldn't work with me so easily, now would it?"

"Excuses, excuses, if it wasn't that easy, then how were you able to kill them before they killed you first?" Phoenix walks out of the kitchen, disgusted, "I'm going in the living room. Both of you are oblivious." Darrell follows Phoenix into the living room and closes the door, "Oh, I'm oblivious?! It's not my fault I got into this damn mess!"

"Well, you fucking believe him! You're just as crazy!"

"Really? I'm not the one that just lashed out on

everybody. You're probably the one that's crazy around here. You can't control yourself, that pretty much sums it up there."

Phoenix starts crying, "Well, I have my reasons why I'm like this! You don't understand!" Darrell saw her tears and gave her a hug, "Hey, I know what it's like, but you have got to snap out of this behavior. You can't let your emotions control you. We can't afford that in a situation like this." Darrell let's go and places his hands on her shoulders, "Now we have to prepare for tomorrow, because they could still be watching us like Rose and Russell said. Are you going to be okay?" Phoenix hesitated, "I still don't trust Russell, but, yeah, I'll be fine."

Darrell and Phoenix hear the kitchen door open. "What's going on?" Adrian said, frustrated.

"It's nothing, Adrian." Russell was leaning on the counter top as his arms were crossed. Adrian walks up to Russell and grabs him, "You know, what the hell is going on with you?" Russell pushes him away, "It's nothing, Adrian. Didn't I say that? You better back the fuck up."

"Fuck you, man. This is why we don't get along. You're pathetic, Russell, how long are you going to pretend? You can't hide forever."

"I hide because you can't learn to shut your fucking mouth."

"Well, maybe you should look in the mirror before you decided to take me with you."

"I'll look when I'm done fucking up your face."

Phoenix whispers to Darrell, "Stay right here."

Russell and Adrian start flying fists and push each other while they break objects in the kitchen.

Phoenix opens the living room door and walks upstairs. "Maybe you should listen more often," Russell said. Adrian punches him in the face and resumes the fight.

Phoenix goes in the computer room and grabs a silver pistol, powered by sizzling hot water. She runs downstairs and fires one round at the kitchen ceiling, startling Russell and Adrian. The smoke was coming out of the barrel as the round almost pierced a hole through the ceiling.

Darrell panicked and ran out of the living room, "What the fuck, Phoenix?!" He sees Russell and Adrian looking at Phoenix, shocked. "Are you crazy?!" Russell yelled. "Are you trying to get us killed?!"

Phoenix was angry, but she was calmer, "As a matter of fact, I am crazy. But if you guys want to get out of this alive, I suggest you guys fucking cool it or both of you are going to be on my hit list! Because I'm not in the mood today, either!"

Russell looks at Adrian in disgust and takes a deep breath. Russell walks away and heads towards the computer room. "We have our differences, Adrian. Remember that," Russell says to himself.

Adrian waves his hand to himself, telling Darrell and Phoenix to follow him in the garage. Darrell closes the kitchen door behind him. "So, what the hell is his problem?" Adrian said.

"Apparently, Rose was his love interest, but failed to

protect her in the first place," Phoenix said.

"He's selfish."

"We kind of figured that," Darrell said.

"Now you see why I don't get along with him." Adrian grabs a rag from the sink. "And another thing, he can't just decide to leave and cause damage to something. He doesn't think at all." Phoenix looks down and says, "We don't really think, either. We're all the same in some way."

"That's very true, I tell myself that every day, but not everybody's the same in the organization."

"What did you originally want to do before they forced you in there?" Darrell said.

"I wanted to be free, just like everybody else. I didn't want to worry about anything at all. But look where I'm at now, I have to be a slave to an asshole that only cares about himself."

"Well, you don't have to be. You have an opportunity to walk out, because you have your whole life ahead of you.

Have you ever thought of sneaking out without telling him?"
Phoenix said.

"I have, hundreds of times. Russell would kick my ass if I
even tried."

"You should hang with us more often. I don't take shit
from the organization at all."

"Well, I know that, don't have to tell me twice," Adrian
laughed.

"We make a perfect team, we have a wheelman, a
shooter, and you like to work on cars, so, there may be
something that's hinting a clue."

"Well, I've always liked working on cars my whole life. At
least the organization was somewhat courteous enough to
select your own position."

"Have you ever heard of B&N Financing?" Darrell said.

"Yeah, it's a multi-billion dollar company, why?"

"That's where Phoenix and I work, or worked. There's a
location in New York City that's large enough and is usually

open for anyone looking for a job. There's plenty of opportunities there, you get paid big on your starting salary."

"I'm not really the guy that looks for money. It's not always about money. I see a different light than what you see."

"Well, everybody has their own taste, so, no hard feelings."

"But since the recovery of the economy, the world was giving people another chance, to start over."

"So, are you in, Adrian? I mean you have helped us before," Phoenix said.

"Not right now. I'm not coming with you guys tomorrow, I just can't. I have something to do, trust me."

Phoenix smiles brazenly, "Why do you always try to get away from us? There's something about you, what is it?"

"I want to be free, Phoenix. That's what our founding fathers wanted for us, right?."

Phoenix shakes her head in affirmation, "Oh, I get it. I like the way you think."

"It's what I've always thought. But, I'm pretty sure that Russell wants you to get some rest for tonight since he wants you out by morning."

"Okay, I guess we will talk to you later. You think about it if you're interested in helping us."

"Oh, I already do a lot of that," Adrian smiles.

As Darrell and Phoenix walk to of the kitchen, Phoenix almost forgot to say something to Adrian. "Oh, and I'm sorry that I threatened you earlier," Phoenix said, smiling.

"Oh, it's cool, I'm used to it. I've dealt with it long enough back at IFHR," Adrian smiles and points at both of them. "You guys get some rest." Darrell and Phoenix walk into the living room and hang out there for the rest of the day.

As the day turns to night, the group rests as they prepare for what's ahead of them for the next day.

<h1 style="text-align:center">Chapter 19: Escape</h1>

August 16, 2020

It is dawn as a loud boom from outside startled Phoenix and Darrell, waking them up. "What the hell was that?" Phoenix said quietly.

"C'mon, guys, let's get moving!" Russell said as he ran past the living room. Phoenix quickly puts on her strap around her back and inserts the assault rifle into it and grabs her pistols. Darrell grabs his pistol beside him. They bolt from the couches and run up to the computer room to stock up on weapons laid out across the table. "Shit!" Phoenix said in frustration as she grabs her leather suit and jacket. "Did a bomb go off or something?"

"Maybe there's something more to it," Darrell said.

Phoenix grabs the swords Rose gave her and looks at her reflection, "Maybe." She places the swords on the back of her hoist. They grab belts for other weapons and place them around their waist. Russell was in the kitchen and yelled, "What are you waiting for? Let's go!" He enters the garage. They hear another boom from outside, shaking the ground. Darrell and Phoenix exit the computer room and bolt towards the kitchen door.

Darrell and Phoenix enter the garage and get into their vehicles. "I'll open the door for you!" Adrian said. He runs to the hand scanner by the sink and presses his hand on it. As the scanner turned green, the door slowly opens. "Maybe we'll see you again one day," Phoenix yelled.

"You guys will meet me again in time, but you need to get out of here. I have something to take care of. For right now, it's not safe here."

"But, what about your safety?" Phoenix said.

"Don't worry. As long as you're hiding, it's easy to blend in under the tension of fire."

"You always were a rookie," Russell said to Adrian. He just looked at Russell in disgust. They hear another loud boom that came from a couple blocks away. Adrian yells, "I'm going to close the door. You should be able to get out of here if you make it quick."

Phoenix said, "But, Adrian, we can't just leave you-"

"Just go! Trust me, they won't find me!"

The group reverses and propel straight onto the road, away from the auto shop as they see the garage door already closing. They were in shock as they saw some of the buildings around them on fire and in smoke. The fire and smoke came from the top of the buildings. Some people were sprinting and looked back as they were yelling in panic. "What the hell's going on? Why are they running?" Phoenix said.

"Keep your eyes peeled," Russell said.

As the group drives through a city block, they see two Arma tanks emerging from the distance behind them. "Shit! We gotta get a move on!" Darrell said. The tanks behind them are moving their turrets in all directions, shooting at buildings and damaging them significantly. They were too far away to see the abandoned auto shop. Phoenix quickly looked back and started to get worried. "Adrian!" she yelled.

Suddenly, two tanks emerged with one from each side, startling the group. "Look out!" she yells. The tanks move their turrets and fire at the buildings closest to them, barely missing the group. "Shit, that was close!" Darrell said.

"We gotta help Adrian, they may have got him!"

"It's no use, Phoenix! How are we supposed to turn around?! There are Arma tanks behind us!" Russell said.

The group looks up at the sky and see a group of five jet fighters speeding past, forming a V pattern. "Are you fucking kidding me?!" Darrell said. The jets begin to disperse. "What are they doing? Are they here to help us?" Phoenix said. The jets drop a cluster of small bombs, decimating small portions of the city. They see the explosions destroying tall buildings in the distance. "It's an air raid!" Darrell said.

"Then let's go!" Phoenix said.

Darrell and Russell go full throttle as they try to outrun the Arma tanks behind them. The tanks constantly fire their artillery as an attempt to take the group down, but they barely miss. Their hearts were racing as they make quick turns around the city. "We can't shake them off, Russell, where are we supposed to go now?!" Darrell said.

"It's not safe to talk about that right now, we have to get out of the city. From the looks of it, it's the only way out!" Russell said.

After narrowly escaping from the wave of tanks and jets, the group successfully exit out of the city limits of Los Angeles. "So, where do we go, Russell?" Phoenix said. Russell takes a deep breath, "There's going to be a secret airbase in Idaho."

"Where at in Idaho?" Darrell said.

"Harriman State Park, Fremont County. They like to find large open areas to hide out in. This time, we're going to lay low on this one. They may be planning something by the time we get there. They're going to have lots of aircraft, mostly the ones we just saw."

"Why do we need to go to an airbase?" Phoenix said.

"Because this time, we're going to fly."

Phoenix looks back to see the city of Los Angeles slowly becoming ruins by IFHR.

Chapter 20: Flight

August 18, 2020

Harriman State Park, Idaho

It was a cloudy day as the clouds were their darkest shade of gray. There was a large opening that showed the lighter clouds in the skies. The group is driving on a state route as they see an airbase that's large in size. There was a large roster that contained jet fighters, bombers, and drone aircraft. "Reduce your speed, we're drawing in towards the base," Russell said. He is wearing his business attire. The base's establishment number was 00484.

The group hangs a turn and goes towards the entrance. They stop as they notice a security touchpad on the side of the entrance's thick steel doors. Russell gets out of his vehicle and runs to the touchpad. He makes a gesture with his hand at Darrell and Phoenix. "Stay right there," Russell yelled. He uses his wrist communicator to override the security lock, emitting its blue glow. The lock beeped three times, granting him access.

The doors slowly opened as Russell walked back to his vehicle. "Be careful, the place may be heavily guarded with these bastards," he said. They slowly drive through the entrance and drive around the parking lot of the base. "We're going to park here, for now, we're going to sneak through the entrance on the other side. Ready your weapons." They get out of their vehicles and walk towards a pair of double doors. Russell whispers, "There's a large fleet of jet fighters parked beside the base. We're going to go in there to get some answers. If we get outnumbered, we're bolting out of there and driving to the nearest plane we see."

The group takes a few steps away from the doors until

they are leaning by the side of them. Russell moves forward and cautiously opens one of the doors. They peeked into the doors, but all there was to see was pitch black. They go inside to enter a long hallway. Russell holds the door open to see what's on the side of him. There was a red glass casing that read, IN CASE OF EMERGENCY, BREAK GLASS. There was a flashlight inside. Russell shatters the glass with his elbow and grabs the flashlight. "That should do the trick," Russell whispers as his voice echoes. He turns it on and shines it in the distance. The light showed pipes in cages on both sides. "This is creepy, I have a bad feeling about this," Phoenix said.

"Shh! Quiet, they could be by the end of the hallway," Russell said.

"Hey, who's out there?" An agent's voice was faintly heard from the other end of the hallway. Russell panics and shines the flashlight on the ground, "Shit!" He hesitates.

"Let's keep going. There are small cubby holes under some of the pipes. Keep going until you find one. We're gonna get this agent coming around from here," Russell added. They keep going until they slide under small openings below the pipes on the sides of the walls. They lay down and lower their weapons. "We're going to ambush him, but do it quietly. There may be more behind him. Get against the wall," Russell said.

An agent emerges from the end of the hallway with a flashlight and walks towards where the group is hiding. "Is anybody here?" he said. He briefly shines his flashlight in both directions and walks past the group. "You're not supposed to be here. If there's someone here, either you get out of here now, or you're going to be in a bad position."

Phoenix slowly crawls out of the cubby hole from where Darrell was in and stands up. She slowly walks to the agent as he has his back turned. Phoenix made a footstep that was loud enough for the agent to turn around. The agent startles and draws his pistol. He is bald and white in skin color. Phoenix charges and punches him hard in the face, causing him to temporarily lose balance and drop his gun, creating a loud metal clang. Russell and Darrell emerge from the cubby holes and run to Phoenix. She grabs the agent and forcefully pushes him against one of the cages, making him fall to the ground and drop his flashlight. He sits as Russell and Darrell draw their pistols at the agent. The agent panics as he's breathing heavily. "Shh! You better calm down right now!" Phoenix said. The agent begins to hyperventilate. "Hey, hey, hey, hey!" Phoenix tries to calm the agent down, but to no avail. She pushes him against the cage with her arm on his neck. "I said calm the fuck down!" The agent slows his breathing, but was still terrified. "Now let's try this again, I usually kill my prey, but this will be an exception. We'll spare you, but if you don't tell us what's going on, we'll kill you right on the spot and leave right now! So tell me, what is your name and what are you planning?"

"I ain't telling you shit," the agent said. Phoenix gets frustrated and pulls one of her pistols out of her pocket in her leather suit. She lightly squeezes on the trigger, "What are you planning?!" The agent starts to get terrified, "Alright, I'll tell you!" Phoenix lowers her pistol and listens to the agent.

"My name is Devin Steele. They're going to plan a threat that's not only on a national level, but globally."

"Where are they heading now?"

Devin sighs and says, "Washington, D.C." Darrell and Phoenix panic as they gasp. "I knew it," Russell said.

"Why the national capital?" Phoenix continued.

"The organization worked in numbers, just like how you guys started your wild goose chase, but things are different now. Ever since you and Darrell narrowly escaped from the brush of death a while back, you guys climbed to the top of the list for IFHR's most wanted targets. You'll find out soon enough when the time comes." Devin looks at Russell, "And as for you, Russell. You assisted the targets, which is a big infraction, but you're not who you say you are. You may have dodged us this time, but you're never going to win."

"I already did," Russell says with a cunning smile.

"*Tst*, we'll see about that. You belong to us." Devin yells loud enough to where it can be heard throughout the hallway, "Guys, I found them!" The group is startled as they quickly stand up. "What the hell is wrong with you?!" Phoenix said.

The group sees a few agents emerging from the end of the hallway. "Oh, you motherfucker!" Phoenix said.

"Let's go, now!" Russell said.

The group turns around and sprint to the double doors. The agents from the distance fire at them, missing by mere inches. Devin gets up and joins the rest of the agents. Russell budges the door as they exit out of the base. Devin fires at the door, just missing Phoenix. "Let's get to a plane now!" Russell said. They get into their vehicles and drive into the long runway and see the vast roster of aircraft that stretches for a few miles. "But, what about our vehicles?!" Phoenix said.

"Some of them you can load stuff in, we'll take one of

those!" They accelerate through the middle of the runway and lay their eyes on a large, gray, metallic, armored fighting jet that has a hatch on the back to load cargo. They see a white McLaren parked beside the back of the base next to the runway. "I'll get in the jet and open the hatch in the back. There's enough room for four people in the cockpit," Russell said.

"Do you even know how to fly a jet?!" Phoenix said.

"Phoenix, I've worked in the organization long enough to fly a jet. It's not that hard." They get out of their vehicles. "Okay, while I open the hatch and start the turbines, you look out for the base just in case they show up."

"Alright, we got this," Darrell said as he and Phoenix were readying their weapons.

"Locked and loaded," Phoenix said.

"When the hatch opens, pull the vehicles into the storage unit. The keys are already in my car. It's unlocked," Russell said. He runs to the front of the jet and gets inside it.

Darrell and Phoenix see the back of the jet slowly lower down, revealing a lit storage unit. The units are capable enough to fit ten vehicles at a time. They notice the same five men including Devin running towards the jet. "After them!" Devin yelled. The agents fire at them as Devin goes after the McLaren. Darrell and Phoenix dive onto the ground and take cover beside their vehicles. Phoenix takes her pistol and fires a couple rounds at one of the agents, killing him instantly. Darrell takes his pistol and fires a round as it disperses during travel. The fragments went through the agents' legs as they yell in agonizing pain. Phoenix finishes the other three agents off by shooting them in the head.

Darrell and Phoenix get into the vehicles and drive up the inclined plane of the hatch into the storage unit. "C'mon, we can't let Devin get away!" Phoenix said.

"You guys get the vehicles in?!" Russell said, his voice was muffled.

"We're good!" Darrell said.

"We still need to get Devin!" Phoenix said.

Darrell and Phoenix run down the inclined plane and repeatedly shoot at Devin's vehicle, sprinting after it. Devin propels through the runway and turns out of it, disappearing from their sight. They stop running as they catch their breath. Phoenix gets angry and stomps her foot in frustration, "Shit, he got away!"

"It's no use! Going after him isn't important right now! The entire nation's on the line! Get inside, there will be suits inside the jet when you're ready! I'll open the front for you! Use the ladder beside it to get on!" Russell said. The hatch closes from the back of the jet.

Darrell and Phoenix run around the jet and climb up the ladder. As they squeeze themselves through the back seats, they see the suits neatly folded with a helmet on top. The suits were all black as there were jackets, gloves, and helmets with a clear sight on the front of them. Russell already has his suit on. He looks at the base to check for other agents, "It looks like we're clear for now, you'll have time. Put those helmets on, too. They'll help you with breathing during flight." They put on their suits as Phoenix looks around in the interior of the jet. "So, this is what it's like in a jet?" Phoenix said.

"Yeah, sometimes it's hard to tell from the outside when identifying what class they are. This is an elite aircraft," Russell said, closing the front of the jet. "Packs a shitload of firepower. It's built for speed, too. It's a modified Lockheed Martin." Darrell and Phoenix are fully suited. The interior contained multiple buttons with an assortment of lighted hues. There is a front and rear screen for aiming at enemies. There were also screens for each person in the back seats that are similar to the front. In the elite class for aerial vehicles, back seat passengers have access to weapons that come with the jet. "Alright, next thing you have to do is connect your helmets to the oxygen systems. You see the tubes in front you? Connect those to the front of your helmets and you'll have oxygen during the flight. Now sit tight, I'm going to activate the turbines," Russell said.

Russell closes the front hatches on the side and activates the turbines as flames come out from the back. The screens turn on after the jet engine was activated. "Right now, you're seeing the front and the back. You have access to part of the weapon systems inside the jet. The heads-up display in front of you shows the ammunition supply, the jet's speed, and the overall condition of the jet. Just like the front seats, only a couple differences." Russell pulls down the dual seat belts and clicks them. "Alright, buckle up and hang on, the thrusts on these Lockheeds are quick as hell, even during takeoff."

Russell pushes the lever halfway next to the yolk to put it in gear. The jet starts to move as he turns until it straightens on the runway. As he pushes the lever all the way, the thrust kicks into high gear as it moves straight on the runway. For the performance aspect, the engine is heavily modified as the speed is roughly around fifty percent higher than regular standards. Russell prepares them, "Get ready, we're going to take off on three!" The jet is traveling at sixty knots, about seventy miles per hour. "Two!" The jet climbs up to speed as it nearly triples. "One!" Russell pulls the yolk towards him. "HANG ON!"

The jet drastically increases altitude and speed as the G-force pushes them back in their seats, mimicking the effects of a centrifuge used for pilots in training. Russell straightens the jet and lowers the speed. The group heavily breathes after experiencing the takeoff. "Holy shit," Darrell said.

"It's alright, you'll get used to it. It'll probably take about a couple hours to get to the capital at top speed. It's just over two thousand miles from where we're at. Best prepare yourself, they may send reinforcements after us. That's the last thing we need on our hands right now."

Darrell and Phoenix look down to see that they're just above cloud level, which is about five miles in the air. "I'll be fucking damned. We're in a fucking jet, this shit is too real," Darrell said.

The group heads to the capital of the United States,

preparing for anything of what the organization has planned

for takeover.

Chapter 21: The Archives

An hour is invested into the flight as the group exits the state of Virginia. The weather is stormy as it is raining and thundering. "We're about three hundred miles away from D.C. They may be coming any minute," Russell said.

Russell sees three black fighter jets with the IFHR insignia drawing in on the side of them. "Get ready," Russell said. "They're closing in fast." One of the black jets fires their machine guns at Russell. He quickly dives higher in the sky and goes in a circle. The jets disperse except for the one shooting at Russell. He straightens the jet and pursues the one firing at him, engaging in a dogfight. "Fire, I have a lock!" Russell said. The group fires missiles at the jet's rear and shoots him out of the sky.

The two remaining jets fire at Russell. He weaves in all directions, attempting to evade them. "I can't shake them off!" he says. One of them shoots a heat seeking missile at the group's jet. "Oh, shit! Russell, do something!" Phoenix said. Russell finds the button for flares and activates them. A few bright flares come out of the rear of the jet. The flares disrupt the lock of the missile. The group fires their machine guns and missiles at one of the jets and blows it out of the sky.

Russell dives into the air once more and follows the last jet to engage a dogfight. He activates the special missiles, which are the Hellfire missiles. IFHR's Hellfire missiles are twice as large and have a higher blast radius than the United States' military standards, totaling up to around two hundred and fifty pounds per missile. He fires a group of four missiles.

The missiles disperse and follow the jet as it tries to evade them. "C'mon! C'mon!" Russell said. The missiles impact the jet, destroying it as it shatters to pieces. "Yes!" Russell said. "It doesn't seem there's any more on our tail. It's safe to land." He activates the thrust to speed up and head for Washington, D.C.

Russell enters Washington D.C. as they see fleets of jets circling around the White House shooting at each other. A couple of the United States military jets were already shot down as a couple IFHR jets were also shot down. Darrell and Phoenix gasp as they look around to see the falling jets. Russell finds a runway near an airport next to the White House, "Don't worry about them, we have to get to land, there's a base that gives us the answers we're looking for. It's going to be located just about a couple miles from the White House."

Russell reduces the thrust as he approaches the runway. He slowly pulls the yolk upward as he loses altitude. "The base will be located at Rock Creek Park. Prepare to drive like a bat out of hell when we get to ground. Don't stop for anything. They may have every type of vehicle out there," Russell said. They touch ground as the jet's wheels come out from the bottom. He successfully stops in the middle of the runway. He opens the hatches on the sides of the jet. They take off their suits as Russell opens the back hatch and get out.

The group bolts out of the jet and get into their vehicles. They back out of the jet and drive through the runway and onto the road, quickly shifting gears. "When you see an enemy, take them down! If they're in your way, shoot through them if you have to!" Russell said. They turn out of the runway and drift onto the highway. They look over to see the grassland of the White House. "Oh, my God," Darrell panicked as he saw a fleet of IFHR jets swarm the large park in front of the White House. All of them fire their machine guns at the people on the sidewalks and grass. They also hit the Washington Monument and part of the White House, but they don't collapse. The jets drop small bombs as they decimate Lafayette Square. They see armored vehicles from IFHR drive through the park that included supercars, trucks, SUVs, and Arma tanks and head for the White House. Police units and military vehicles emerge as they drive past the perimeters of the White House, creating a standoff between IFHR and themselves. The two sides start battling, turning the park into a massive kill zone. "Please, God, be with us," Darrell said to himself, terrified.

Two supercars come from behind as they drive beside the group. Darrell and Russell ferociously rammed them to their sides as they hit the barriers of the highway, making them fall off of it. They take a left and drive into oncoming traffic as they go down an exit. The group is now on ground level.

The group accelerates as they are side by side with each other. They notice a large roadblock in the distance held by IFHR. "Use the mortars!" Russell said. They both activated the mortars and aim them at the center of the roadblock. They shoot the vehicles as they leave a devastating explosion, destroying the roadblock.

As the group speeds through the roadblock, two Arma tanks drive towards them, shooting at the buildings on their sides. They also notice two more tanks coming from behind them. "We gotta get a move on, there's more!" Darrell said. They shoot the mortars at the tanks in front of them. The Arma tanks' armor was barely affected, but the dual tracks were blown off, spreading small pieces of gears and metal on the road. "Their dual tracks are their weakness!" Russell said.

"Get in front of me, Russell. Go ahead of me," Darrell said. Phoenix panics, "What?! Are you crazy, Darrell?! What do you think you're doing?!"

"I'm going to get rid of the tanks behind us." Russell turns and gets in front of Darrell and propels off. Darrell slows down and switches to first gear as he approaches the damaged tanks. He looks down at the buttons for the weapon systems and presses the horseshoe magnet. The screen detects the tanks' magnetic poles as north. Darrell switches his current pole to south and sets the power to 40%. "I hope this works," Darrell said. As he drives in between the Arma tanks, the screen detected the magnetic poles. He immediately activated the magnetism and slowly pulls the tanks towards him. The tanks from behind shoot at Darrell, but they nearly miss. As he accelerates, he pulls the Arma tanks until they are sitting sideways across from each other and turns off the magnetism. Darrell accelerates to catch up with Russell.

The pursuing tanks were moving too fast to react to the damaged ones. They hit the damaged tanks and explode, creating a shockwave and destroying everything around it. "Go faster, the explosion's getting bigger!" Phoenix said.

"I'm doing my best, Phoenix!" The explosion stopped growing, but there were a couple vehicles flying in the air, falling towards Darrell. He notices them and activates the nitrous. He moves from lane to lane to avoid colliding with other vehicles. He sees Russell and loses distance with him. Darrell turns and drives beside Russell. "Took you long enough," Russell said.

"Wasn't easy," Darrell said.

After the group drives for three more miles, they come across a large, black base as they were roaming in Rock Creek in the middle of nowhere. The base's establishment number was 00113. There were barely any trees as it was out in the open. The outer perimeters of the base were surrounded by blacktop for other parked vehicles.

The group stops in front of the entrance of the base as there were steel double doors. Russell quickly types in the combination on the touchpad and unlocks the doors. They push open the doors and enter a dimly lit, long, narrow hallway. They start running as they see a few agents armed with assault rifles, making them stop running. "Hello, guys," one of the agents said. They aim at the group. "We meet again." The group shoots at the agents as they kill all but one. Phoenix charges at the agent and punches him in the head and turns around his back. She elbows him in the back of his skull. Russell charges at him and twists his head, cracking his neck and killing him.

The group looks around as they enter a brightly lit hallway. "Here's the plan, you go left, I'll go right. We'll split up from here," Russell said.

"Wait, where are you going?" Phoenix said.

"We're done from here, we each have our own unfinished business. You have yours, I have mine, but yet, have the same goal. To kill these bastards and be free. It's been nice working with you."

"You were an asshole, anyway." They look at each other one more time. "Now, go, they'll be coming any minute," Russell said.

"Come on, Darrell, let's go," Phoenix said. They run to their doors as Darrell and Phoenix enter another room. The room they entered in had boxes, lockers, and crates. There was a black stairwell in the distance that goes to another floor. There was a black metallic platform that stretches across the room. A door was budged open from the platform above them as a group of agents swarms out with assault rifles, aiming at them. "Stay right there! Your time has been up a long time ago! You ready to finally rest on your deathbed?!" said one of the agents.

Darrell and Phoenix look at each other. "Remember in training?" Phoenix said.

"You almost fucking killed me, but yeah," Darrell said.

"You still owe me from saving your ass multiple times."

They aim at the agents. "Let's finish this!" Phoenix said. She pulls out her assault rifle and fired at the agents, killing a couple of them. Darrell pulls his pistol out and fires a couple rounds, also killing a couple more. She and Darrell run under the platform as the agents fire their weapons. The agents run down the stairs and go after them.

Darrell and Phoenix charge at the agents. Darrell starts a brawl against three of the agents as Phoenix only focuses on one. An agent grabs Phoenix's arm and squeezes it with a tight grip. She takes her free arm and hits his pressure point by his neck, making him jerk his head sideways. She breaks free from his grip and unsheathes one of her swords. She chops the agent's hand off as he yells in pain. The blood was gushing out as part of the bone was showing. She slashes him in the neck as blood squirts from his veins and falls to the floor, gurgling to his death.

Phoenix ran towards the stairs and readies her pistol as she sees more agents coming out. She clings onto a wall and performs a wall run. While wall running, she still holds the sword as she has the pistol in her other hand. She slashes the agent running down the stairs and shoots at a couple on the platform. She jumps off of the wall and kicks an agent in the face and sets foot on the platform.

Phoenix puts away her pistol and unsheathes her other

sword. The agents on the platform all aim at her. She gets into a defensive stance, forming an X with the swords. One of the agents charge at her. She quickly gets out of the stance and cut through him deeply with both swords. The rest of the agents fire at her as she blocks a couple bullets, deflecting them back and killing a couple agents. The three remaining agents on the platform stop firing and use their guns as melee weapons against her. She blocks them and cuts one of them in the leg. The one that's cut falls on his back. Phoenix kills the agent by taking both swords and cutting through his diaphragm. She pulls out the swords and focuses on the two agents. The agents charge and constantly block each other's strikes. As the agents were distracted, Phoenix saw her chance to attack. She disperses the swords and slices both agents in the chest at the same time. Both agents thud on the platform and lay there motionlessly.

Phoenix focuses her attention on the agents on the ground. The three agents have Darrell pinned down. He grunts and yells, "Phoenix, do something!" One of the agents bashes him with his assault rifle and says, "You better shut up and sit tight, boy! This will only take a minute!"

Phoenix pulls out her pistol and aims at the agents. She takes a deep breath and holds the gun steadily. She aims at the agents' heads. She quickly fires a round in each of the agents' heads and kills them. Darrell was shocked and pushes their dead bodies as he gets up. Phoenix smiles with confidence, "Just like in training." She spins the pistol by the trigger and puts it in her leather suit. "Now get up here, there may be something you might want to see."

Darrell runs up the steps and follows Phoenix. They walk into a hallway that is filled with steel cabinets that are arranged from A to Z. "Start opening the cabinets, there's gotta be a clue why these people decided to form such a corrupted syndicate that nobody really knows," Phoenix said.

"People talk about it, it's a constant topic in today's media, but nobody knows the real truth behind it," Darrell said.

"Until that person finds out themselves."

"That's why I don't like following conspiracies, I've had other things to worry about long before I got into all of this." Darrell opens the cabinet with the letter, M. The cabinets go by last names as there is more than one cabinet with the same letter with some of them. He sees a series of thick manila folders and pulls one of them out. He opens the folder to reveal printed documents and crouches down. He's shocked as the portrait reveals the same man that was kidnapped in the previous year. "Phoenix, come here, you're not going to believe this," Darrell said.

"What is it?" she grabs a folder out of one of the cabinets and walks up to him. She crouches down as Darrell points at the man's portrait. "Does that ring a bell?" Darrell said.

"Wait, that's the man that was reported missing in-"

"2019? Yes I know, I read the article in the newspaper that year." He looks closely at the status below the portrait section. "His name's Francesco Maldonado. Date of birth:

April 25, 1976. Cancellation Number: 386419373."

"Cancellation number?" Phoenix said. "They did work in numbers, but how did they get away with it?"

"Terminated July 19, 2019." Something pops up in Darrell's head. "Wait a minute!"

"What?"

"That's the same day he was reported missing! That would also mean that he knew what was coming to him!"

"Do you think he could be alive?"

"He's not alive."

"How could he not be alive? Maybe he is."

"I assure that he's not alive. If he was alive, he'd be in the same situation we're in, but it was too late for him, they already canceled him out. They wouldn't be after us if he was still alive. They would still be after him until he was dead, just like us! I'm surprised we even got this far!"

Phoenix lays her folder down on the ground, "I found this in the L section." She opens it up to reveal her name,

"Phoenix Leyton. Maiden Name: Hadaway." She was surprised when she saw her maiden name. "They even keep all of your personal history! How the fuck do these people do it? These people are sick!" She resumes reading her status. "Date of Birth: March 31, 1993. Cancellation Number: 614876950." She gasps, "Warren, he's gotta be in here." She looks further into the folder and finds his name. "Warren Leyton. Date of Birth: March 17, 1993. Cancellation Number: 757866362. Terminated: July 21, 2019." She started to get angry, "But he wasn't even a target! This doesn't make sense! He was part of the organization! Why would they kill off their own kind in the first place?!"

Darrell suddenly gets up from the ground, "Where's F?" He walks around the cabinets until he finds the F section. He pulls a folder out and lays it on the ground. "Friegman's gotta be in here." He looks through the folder until he finds his name, "Darrell Friegman. Date of Birth: February 15, 1993. Cancellation Number: 723547461." He notices a stamped mark on the document reading CURRENT TARGET. He gasps and tenses up, "Phoenix, let me see yours."

Darrell walks to Phoenix and crouches down near her, "Let me see your portrait." He looks at the bottom of her document and saw the same stamp on his. "But you're not a target, either!"

"I helped you, that's the thing. That's why they're after me, too," Phoenix said.

"Let's look through the folders. There may be something that could lead to somewhere." They skimmer through the folders as they contained a max of up to a couple hundred documents in each folder. "Looks like they don't go past people that are born in the 1960s, 1969 specifically." The organization does not go after people that have already reached their fiftieth birthday. "The youngest person I can find in here has a birth year of 1998." The youngest a person can be registered for a cancellation number has to reach their twenty-first birthday.

"Oh, my God," Darrell said in panic. Most of the targets'

statuses come up as terminated. "About half of these people in this folder are already dead." He gets angry, "At least they have the goddamn courtesy to care enough for children and seniors!" He stands up and punches one of the cabinets. "What the FUCK is going on?!"

Phoenix looks ahead of her to notice a door, "What's that door over there?"

Darrell calms down, "What door?"

"The door ahead of us." She gets up and walks towards the direction of the door. "There might be something in there. Let's go check it out. Ready your weapons just in case they decide to show up."

Darrell and Phoenix run to the door and budge through it, only to enter another hallway. They notice two agents laying motionless on the ground, the same ones that were killed four days before they met Russell. "There's another door up ahead. Let's make a run for it." They sprint to the end of the hallway and stop when they reach the dead agents.

"Hmm, apparently they're too lazy to clean up after themselves," Phoenix said. The agents' bodies were slightly reduced down as their hair appeared longer from the prolonged stages of death. After some time when death occurs, the human body usually causes the skin to dry up, making it feel like the texture of gloves.

Darrell and Phoenix slowly walk over the bodies. The bodies left a strong odor. However, the halls were clean enough, which surprisingly attracted no insects. Phoenix reacts to the stench and covers her hand over her nose, "These guys fucking stink. How long have they been laying here?"

Darrell covers his nose, "A while, maybe a month. Fucking animals they are." He puts his hand on the hand scanner by the door. The holographic screen read ACCESS DENIED. He tries again, but gets the same result. "Shit!" he said, hitting a wall. He looks down at the bodies as his face cringes, "We're going to have to use one of the bodies."

"Are you fucking kidding me?!" Phoenix said, disgusted.

Darrell carefully picks up one of the bodies and pulls it to the scanner. Due to the body's prolonged stage of rigor mortis, it was hard to move the agent's arm. A couple of the bones break as Darrell places the agent's hand on the scanner. He forces the hand down, breaking the agent's wrist. The scanner was detecting the material, but the access was denied. "Shit!" Darrell yelled. "The bodies are too decomposed!" He takes the body and kicks it out of his way. "Now, what are we going to do?!"

Phoenix opens the door next to the other agent's dead body. "Darrell, you might want to come look at this," Phoenix said, terrified.

Darrell slowly walks to the door, "What is it?"

"There's more dead bodies."

The room was lit as it showed a few dead bodies scattered around. There were four of them. All of them have holes in their head as they appeared to be gunshots. All of them had their eyes open. "What the fuck?" Darrell said,

shaking and terrified.

"Rose was right, they do take it as a bloodsport. This

looks like a hospital room." One of the agents was laying on a

gurney as he was hanging halfway over it, but wasn't

strapped in. The rest of them were sitting on the ground next

to a countertop with their legs spread out. Darrell walks to

the agent on the gurney and takes his arm as it was moving

freely. "This one was recently killed, but how?" Darrell said.

"Maybe they killed themselves, or somebody killed

them, who knows?"

"This one has been dead for possibly a few minutes."

"If they've been dead for a few minutes, then how were

they killed so quickly?"

"I don't know," Darrell hesitates. He quickly snaps into

reality. "But that doesn't matter right now, we need to find

out what's behind that door. Take one of his arms and put it

over your shoulder. We're using him to get through the door."

They both take his arms and carry him to the hand scanner.

Darrell places the agent's hand on the scanner as it's being detected. "How do you know this will work?" Phoenix said.

"They may have worked in this specific base." The screen shows the words, ACCESS GRANTED. Darrell grabs the body and pushes it aside next to one of the other dead bodies. They push open the door and reveal a room that's almost pitch black. They walk on the steep platform that's suspended from what seems to be a bottomless pit. They look around as the walls were far away from the platform. "Wow, I've never seen anything like this," Phoenix said in awe.

Darrell and Phoenix notice a large holographic screen in the distance. They notice that their names and portraits are on there side by side. They walk on the wider platform and look up. "That's us," Phoenix said. "Why do they want us so much?"

"Let's let Russell know." Darrell speaks through his

communicator, "Russell, we found the archives. They're in a computer room." No response. "Russell, do you copy? Come in." Still no response.

Suddenly, parts of the walls light up as a loud alarm goes off. Darrell and Phoenix realize that the walls also have holographic screens as they project the same one as the large screen. Darrell and Phoenix tense up. "Let's get the fuck out of here!" Phoenix yelled. They run out of the room and enter the hallway. "This is fucked up," Darrell said. They sprint through the hallways and run down the stairs, exiting the room with the dead agents. They enter the hallway they came in and exit the base.

As Darrell budges through the door in the narrow hallway, they notice Russell with a devious smile standing with a few other agents. They have their arms behind their back, looking at the base. The agents between him had batons.

"Russell, what are you doing?!" Phoenix yelled.

"I've been waiting for a moment like this," Russell said.

Phoenix is shocked and becomes enraged, "I KNEW I shouldn't have trusted you! You're a traitor!"

"Traitor? If I was traitor, I would've been decommissioned by now. I'm finally getting my way with things around here."

"How do you sleep at night, huh? Does it feel good when you kill off innocent people, even your own kind?"

"Yeah, it makes me feel free. I'd like to thank President Lavensa on that one."

"You'll never get away with this, motherfucker!" Phoenix charges at Russell.

"I already did. Agents, grab them!" The three agents between Russell charge at Phoenix and Darrell and start beating them. They are stunned as they are hit in their diaphragm and back. They hit them both in the head with one final blow. They both collapse unconsciously to the ground. The agents walk away from them. "Looks like my work here is done. Pick them up and set them into the base. Good job, people," Russell said.

Russell gets into his vehicle and drives away from the base. The agents drag them back into the base and take them into the hallway Russell went into.

Chapter 22: Rogue

March 18, 2021

"..... I don't really have anywhere to sit, so I might as well sit with you..... Wow, the people here are very nice!..... New York City is such a big city. It's bigger than what some people think..... Looks like you win the game..... Brings back old memories..... Just tell us and we'll do it, just don't kill us!..... Are you one of them?!..... Warren's beside Barrett.....

WARREN!..... I promised to him that I will find a way to put an end to this..... And I will make sure that motherfucker pays..... Just face it, Barrett. Your number's up!..... We have to be careful with what we're going up against. We just met the guy, Darrell..... No matter how many missions we go on, I'm still going to keep my eye on him..... But we can help you, Rose. You still have a chance to be free again!..... If you loved her, you should've brought her with you along with Adrian!..... Go faster, the explosion's getting bigger!..... I helped you, that's the thing..... How long have they been laying here?..... Wow, I've never seen anything like this..... I KNEW I shouldn't have trusted you!..... You'll never get away with this, motherfucker!"

"I already did. Agents, grab them!"

Phoenix slowly opens her eyes and wakes up as her vision was blurry. She blinked a couple times in order to gradually regain her vision. She sees a ceiling light shine down above her. "It was just a dream," she said to herself. "Is it finally over?" She tries to move her body around, but she can barely move. There's nothing that's restraining her. "Why can't I fucking move?" She realized she just woke up from a coma. She didn't have her leather suit on her nor her weapons. She's in a white hospital gown and is wearing only a bra and underwear.

Phoenix tries to move her arms, but she feels like they're being weighed down from an invisible force. She starts talking to herself again, "Okay, Phoenix. Start with your head and arms, then work down to your legs." She starts to rhythmically move her arms and head back and forth to get back some of her movement. She hears the voices of agents coming by the steel door with a glass window in its center. She stops moving and closes her eyes as the agents approach the door. They were carrying assault rifles. They stand by the door and look at her for a moment. "She's still unconscious. Let's check Darrell's room," one of the agents said. They walk away from the door.

Phoenix moves her entire body to get some motion back. She realizes she's on a hospital bed as there was an intravenous bag hooked up to her. There was also a machine that shows her heart and respiratory rate. She grunts as she slowly moves her arm by her other arm and pulls out the tube from the intravenous bag. She slowly moves her legs off of the bed and thuds to the ground. While laying, she looks around the room. All of the walls were white as there was a table in front of her, carrying her weapons. Her suit was hanging by the hospital bed.

She attempts to get up on her feet, but tumbles to the ground. She tries again and gets up, but her body is swaying back and forth. "Come on, get your balance," she said to herself. She stops trying to walk as her body stops swaying. "There you go. Now take slow steps." She walks to the table to grab her pistols, assault rifle, and waist belt for her daggers and knives. She looks to the side to find her swords sheathed up against a wall next to her suit. She quickly takes off her gown and works her way towards her suit. She slowly puts on her suit and sheathed her swords behind her back. She equips the rest of the weapons on her body and clips the belt around her waist. She goes back to the counter and picks up her ear microphone and communicator. She rubs her hands together, "Okay, body's back in shape now. Mostly, at least." She walks to the door and cautiously opens it.

Phoenix enters a brightly lit hallway as there were blue lines going across the center of the walls. She hears the agents from another hallway, making her cling against the edge of a wall. She peeks to see the agents looking through the door of another room. "Darrell's still unconscious," one of the agents said. They walk away from the room and disappear into another hallway.

Phoenix gets off of the wall and walks to Darrell's room. She slowly opens the door and enters inside. "Darrell?" Phoenix said. Darrell was just waking up from his coma in the hospital bed. He was wearing nothing else but a hospital gown and a pair of black dress pants and socks. "Darrell, are you okay?"

"Where am I?" Darrell said.

"We're inside one of IFHR's bases. It looks like a hospital, but I can't say that for sure. You just woke up from a coma.

You have to learn how to walk again to get up."

"How long have I been out?"

Phoenix looks down on her communicator and projects the holographic screen. "Oh, my God," she was shocked.

"How long have we been knocked out for?"

Phoenix looks into Darrell's eyes with terror, "Seven months."

TO BE CONTINUED

Writer's Note

The message in this installment explored the theme of trust and violence. This was a more darker experience throughout the time I invested in writing this. Trust is one of the most important factors in our lives, but once it's broken, it could cause a spark towards a massive chain of events that can be unfolded right in front of your eyes.

Violence is a major factor in the growing problems of our planet. It can range from a small misdemeanor to sadistic tendencies such as a cold-blooded murder. It is a growing sickness that we all know about, but it sometimes goes unspoken. Although the works in this book are entirely fictional, there are several events relating to horrific acts of violence. Most of them go untold. It's a very scary and serious topic to think about. Cherish your life with the ones you love and care about dearly. Live like there's no tomorrow because you may never know what could happen. Because if a sudden impact creates a devastating turn of events, you may never get a chance to see them again.

Hello to anyone who has read this! For those that have not heard of me, my name is Travis Heeter. I am from the town of Vienna, Ohio in Trumbull County. I am an author and a musician. I self-published my first book, The Number Conspiracy on November 22, 2013 while still in high school. I started playing music at the age of 13 and eventually went into singing at the young age of 17 years old. After graduation, I started playing in venues around the Cleveland area with plans to expand in the future.

The Alphabet Archives talked about serious topics as did the previous installment, expect it had a darker setting. My goal with music and writing is to spread awareness about the more serious and controversial topics that most rarely or never touch base on. I am not afraid to dig into the trenches of our disturbing reality of major happenings. With my works, I hope to inspire you, whoever is reading this, to be a messenger, a fighter, and an advocate against the harsh reality of today's world.

Check out my social pages and spread the word!

www.facebook.com/OfficialTravisHeeter

www.reverbnation.com/travisheeter

www.twitter.com/_TravisHeeter_

www.facebook.com/TheNumberConspiracy